WILD MAGIC

Book One of the Wild Magic Series

Wild Magic
(Book One of the *Wild Magic* book series)

Wildwood Publishers
Spirit of the Wildwood, LLC
wildwoodpublishers.com

Cover design: Aimée Cree Dunn.

Graphic design: Aimée Cree Dunn.

Character and scenery images generated by AI (Adobe Firefly, MagicMedia, ImagineMe, Ideogram) and edited by Aimée Cree Dunn. Bagwaji-inini edited by Linda Cree.

All writing is 100% human by Aimée Cree Dunn (aka Nateera Skye).

Various people and sources (including Le Chat by Mistral AI) were consulted regarding Québécois speech patterns, literal language translations, and idiomatic expressions.

ISBN 978-1-970350-07-4

Contact: nateeraskye@outlook.com
         NateeraSkye.com
         WildMagicSeries.com

WILD MAGIC

Book One of the Wild Magic Series

Nateera Skye

Dedicated to my beloved family:

For all you are, for all you do.
You'll always be my favorite wildlings.

Praise...[for] all Thy creatures...especially Brother Sun...he is beautiful and radiant in all his great splendor...

...for Sister Moon and the Stars...clear and precious and beautiful...

...for Brother Wind, for the air and the clouds, for the clear weather and every kind of weather through which Thou gives sustenance to Thy creatures...

...for Sister Water, who is very useful and humble and precious and chaste...

...for Brother Fire...handsome and playful and robust and strong...

...for our sister, Mother Earth, who sustains and guides us....

- Saint Francis of Assisi
"Canticle of the Sun" or "Canticle of the Creatures"
Church of San Damiano, Assisi, Italy
1224/1225 A.D.

Part One

The Hidden Mountains

Chapter One

Long hair billowing in the stormy winds, Moira knelt at Tristan's side where he'd fallen in a small ravine at the base of a craggy hill. His wound was a fatal one. In their storming all the barren highlands seemed to keen with her. Her cheek against his shoulder, Tristan's soul passed over. Moira held him close, running a hand over his long, rain-darkened hair. Salty rivulets of her tears watered the soil, mingling with his blood and the rainfall.

Even as Moira held him, Tristan's body shifted silently, slowly into shards of refracted light. Jumping to her feet, ND2111111111111111

"Pyxi!" Face stern despite the quivers teasing at the corners of her mouth, Ravyn narrowed her eyes.

The beautiful, long-haired, tortoiseshell cat, having politely wended her way around and about Ravyn's ankles for the last ten minutes only to be ignored, casually draped herself over the computer keyboard. Large green cat eyes blinked slowly. Pyxi stretched her black paw, the one guilty of the recent keyboard antics, and yawned.

In a gentle, well-practiced maneuver, Ravyn scooped her feline friend into her lap.

A soft purr slowly rumbled into life.

The deadline was only minutes away. The expectations from the magazine were not high. Drama. Romance. Magic. Sluice those three around a bit each issue and a different concoction always came together.

Eyes shut the better to see, Ravyn swiftly resumed her typing.

The ground shook as the scent of fresh earth mingled with the heavy smell of blood. A seedling broke through where Tristan had lain, a single green leaf thrust upward. In a few heartbeats, the seedling transformed into a sapling which quickly morphed into a young oak. Its trunk grew rapidly in girth. Its limbs pushed outward. Within moments, the tree was massive.

Then all was still, the only movement the oak leaves trembling in the rain.

Snowflakes drifted in the moonlit night beyond the window. The lower glass panes reflected Ravyn's fingers as they flew with near-perfect accuracy over the laptop keyboard weaving a familiar web of words.

This web had kept out the world since she was a small girl curling up in a woodsy nook at recess, pushing back glasses as they slipped off her nose, and reaching for her latest library book while other kids dodged balls, tagged friends and did whatever other loud and rowdy things they liked to do.

Like her father who preferred delving into history rather than paying much mind to contemporary reality, the broader happenings of the day had always seemed best kept at bay. The world got along just fine without her.

However, though as unsuspecting as the rest of us, Ravyn wasn't as inconsequential as she liked to think. She had yet to know it, but her quiet existence as a nearly unheard-of writer making a life in Michigan's wild and wintry Upper Peninsula was about to be shaken to its very roots.

Hand against the trunk of the tree, a slight smile played across Moira's face as spears of grass and tiny red flowers unfurled from the base of the oak like swelling and twisting rivers crossing the once barren land in all directions, fusing life into the wetness of the sodden moors.

So it had begun. The forest groves would be renewed.

Tristan had promised that. She didn't understand how. She didn't understand much of what had happened at all these last few months. But he had promised this.

And he had promised her they'd be together again, reuniting on the other side. Eventually.

A lifetime, though, was a very long time to wait.

Ravyn fumbled for a nearby Kleenex box, grabbed a tissue, and blew her nose. Writing soppy romances, no matter how extreme or ridiculous the melodrama, had its hazards. A red nose and puffy eyes were often hers. A brisk swipe from the back of her hand, though, and the tears were gone.

That done, she opened her work email, wrote something brief to her editor, uploaded the story file, and hit send before minimizing her inbox and pushing the laptop aside. The story wasn't quite what she wanted it to be, but it was what it was.

She glanced at the clock. Shaving the deadline – again – but at least they always got the story before it was due. Maybe only seconds before, but prior to nonetheless.

The computer beeped – almost immediately. Quick and efficient – that was Bev. The woman never slept. Or so it seemed. Assuming it was the usual prompt confirmation that her story had been received, Ravyn didn't even bother to check the message.

Unfolding long legs, Ravyn slipped stockinged feet into fluffy sasquatch slippers and shuffled to a tiny fridge tucked neatly away in a little nook. She'd hid it there so as not to disturb the tower-garret's fairytale ambience. Miniature, perfectly placed string lights and scented candles illuminated the room's warm wood tones, their glow reflecting in the long, arched, and rather drafty windows.

Ravyn's home was a tiny, some might unkindly say dilapidated, nineteenth century home which was cozy most winter days with warmth from a fieldstone fireplace and chocolate aroma from a cake or cookies freshly baked. She was only a stone's throw from her rather fey mother and father, and just down the maple-lined street from her lifelong and most loyal of friends, Kaye.

Nestling in a small town near the foot of the Hidden Mountains, for years the house had been home to Ravyn, her wise and apparently ageless tortoiseshell cat, and many beautiful, sometimes quite extraordinarily ordinary, botanical companions. Like the dandelions rescued from the town's autumn sidewalk expansion project. That's not mentioning the more exotic mimosa, avocado tree, and precious orchid or two.

Her most recent fledgling piece of fiction now resting easy in her editor's inbox, Ravyn settled back on the futon. Fluffy pillow propped precisely at the small of her back, she snuggled under a softly warm blanket and slowly worked her way through a giant bowl of yogurt topped with mandarin oranges, ruminating on what her next story might be.

Pyxi leaped up on quiet cat paws beside her, purr lulling Ravyn bit by bit into a deep drowse. "Just a few minutes of shut-eye," Ravyn murmured, setting the bowl on the floor and drifting moments later into sleep.

It seemed in no time at all the phone downstairs shrilled in a sudden and persistent way, summoning Ravyn from the depths of a dream she couldn't quite recall. There had been wind. Woods. And an intriguing, shifting sort of shadow looming in the blowing snow.

Eyelids heavy, it took effort to open them. Bright sunlight reflected starkly off the the very real, snowy landscape outside. Ravyn swallowed, mouth dry. The bowl that had held yogurt last night sat beside the futon, clearly licked empty to a sparkling sheen, but Pyxi was nowhere to be seen.

The telephone rang again.

"Alright, alright." Ravyn pushed to her feet. Stumbling to the spiral staircase, she stopped to stretch briefly then hurried down the winding stairs, careful of the loose metal step halfway along.

The landline pierced the quiet once more, seeming even more strident than before as if insisting four rings far exceeded sufficient warning of an incoming call.

Before she could reach the phone, however, her decades-old answering machine took over. Ravyn slowed her pace as she neared the telephone stand. Maybe by the time the message ran its course, she'd be awake enough to understand it.

Chapter Two

Phone calls were usually unwelcome intrusions into Ravyn's quiet realm, especially as so often they were simply someone soliciting something – a gadget she didn't need, personal information she didn't want to give, or a candidate she didn't believe would create a brighter future for everyone.

But every once in a while something intriguing came through.

Like today. As she was about to find out.

The ring of the phone having lapsed into silence, Pyxi leaped up next to where it sat on its stand. The answering machine whined on tinny speakers through Ravyn's rather long-winded greeting. Ravyn herself listened with a shoulder slumped against the wall, forehead pressed to its spackled surface, only dimly aware of the wind howling outside around the corners of her home. Eyes closed, she snatched at remnants of sleep while she waited. It had been such a strange dream.

"Ravyn," came a familiar voice from the machine.

Ravyn straightened at its tone, eyes forced open.

It was her editor. "Meeting at the office? Now. You got my email."

Slowly reaching for the phone, Ravyn hesitated before her hand darted quickly forward and lifted the receiver. She couldn't recall the last time they'd met outside of a video conference or email. In-person was reserved for the particularly important things.

Like raises, promotions.

Or, though she wasn't about to dwell on it, the opposite.

Quietly clearing her throat as she brought the phone to her ear, Ravyn's voice came out bright and alert. So she hoped. "Hey, Beverly."

"I didn't wake you." It was more a reprimand than a courteous inquiry. Before Ravyn had the opportunity to answer, however, Bev pushed on. "We have a very important – " She paused to emphasize those last two words. "Meeting right now. The email I sent you last night?"

So she should have checked her inbox.

Beverly's exhalation came across clearly even on the phone. "You can't make it up here now. Obviously."

"Maybe I..." Ravyn's half-hearted suggestion faded. Corporate was over an hour away. Not that she was complaining.

"Never mind. I'll send a conference link. Be on in five." Bev hung up.

Ravyn stared at the phone before replacing the receiver. Phone. Meeting. Webcam. Right. She smoothed her clothes. At least she wasn't in pjs. The pink plaid flannel shirt and black turtleneck with yoga pants would do alright. Rumpled, sure, but it's not like Beverly would notice such things in a video meeting.

Though maybe she'd ditch the flannel for the more professional look of the turtleneck.

Four minutes, a squirt of toothpaste, and a hasty bun later, her relaxed but rather wild black curls escaping almost as quickly as they were tamed, Ravyn was teleconferencing in to something that would change her life forever. At the time, though, she simply wished she could be there in person, at least for nothing else but to sample a little from the array of donuts at the conference table.

That was her first impression.

Her second was the realization that everyone was there, including the other remote writers like herself. Apparently this meeting wasn't going to be about something exclusively personal. The hum of conversation in the room came ragged over the laptop mic. Little was decipherable, though, and nothing held clues as to the reason behind it all.

The only person on the video call, Ravyn diluted the tension noodling around with different avatars wishing she had the moxie to show up for the meeting in such a disguise.

It was a relief when her best friend Kaye, like a familiar cup of tea poured into a favorite mug, suddenly appeared across the miles of fiber optic cable making her way to one of the executive chairs around the table. She settled next to the webcam, her face growing large as she drew close enough to the mic for whispers. "Worried?" she asked Ravyn, biting into a chocolate-frosted long john.

Ravyn shrugged. "Guess we'll see if I should be."

"Everyone thinks, well…" She raised her eyebrows. "It's something big. Could be exciting. Or depressing."

"Big?" Ravyn echoed. "As in, people are going to get fired?"

Kaye shrugged, grimacing. "That'd be the depressing option." She finished her donut.

"The secretaries going to be okay?"

"I hope so."

"They can't let any writers go. There's hardly enough of us to make a monthly mag as it is." Ravyn laughed then sobered. "They wouldn't. Would they?"

"I'm sure you're right," Kaye said. But her smile was tight.

A cold draft crept in from behind, stirring tendrils of Ravyn's hair. The back door creaked open as it so often did if unlocked while strident winds blew outside. Quickly padding over, she lifted the knob just so, snugging the door into place, firmly closing out the chill.

Turning back to the laptop screen, Ravyn saw Beverly had entered the room and was standing at the head of the table, chewing her fingernails. Ravyn frowned. Bev was not a nail nibbler.

One of her assistants walked in, a sheaf of file folders in his arms. They held a whispered consultation. Bev glanced through the top few then handed them back. The assistant left.

The donuts on the table were disappearing quickly although the generally health conscious crew usually eschewed anything more calorie dense than a mini-bagel. Ravyn felt the urge to munch on something too. Before she could make a dash for the kitchen, however, Beverly coughed discreetly. The room's hum of conversation faded completely.

Ravyn's mouth felt parched.

Remaining on her feet, Beverly was quiet, her gaze taking them all in at once. "I'm going to tell it to you straight," she said, leaning on the table, arms rigid. Then she looked at each in turn, even Ravyn through the webcam. "Corporate has sold the magazine. As of today, MegaLit, Inc. owns it. Everyone stays. No one's losing a job. Most of you will continue in the same or similar positions. And as of last night, you all received five percent pay raises from our new management. Those of you who've been assigned to new positions may find an even greater increase."

"New positions?" someone echoed from the otherwise stunned circle around the conference table.

Bev nodded. "Look for an email late tonight with details on how you'll be impacted. Most won't notice much difference. Those changing positions - they'll want to meet with each of you. Some will be meeting partners for revised assignments."

Ravyn's jaw clenched. A hubbub of startled conversation, along with a dozen questions aimed at their editor-in-chief, rose quickly in the room.

"MegaLit?" Kaye whispered over the computer mic, but Ravyn could only shrug. It wasn't a company she'd heard of before.

Beverly held up a hand.

"Did you know, Bev?" someone bravely threw into the gathering quiet.

Lips pressed together, Bev gave her head a short, decisive shake in the negative. "It was a sudden acquisition."

Everyone waited, hoping for additional info, even if it was only another crumb. Someone reached for the last donut.

"Those are really all the details I can share right now." Beverly paused and looked around the room once more. "You'll have emails soon," she promised and adjourned the meeting.

People left fitfully in small groups, voices low.

"Ravyn, stay a bit, will you?" Beverly asked, her voice clear enough to carry over the scattered conversations.

Trying to post a thumbs-up, Ravyn accidentally launched a storm of space rocket emojis instead.

Kaye lifted her eyebrows, trying not to laugh. "Call me later," she said, standing to leave.

Elegant and petite, Bev made her way to the webcam and sat down, folding her hands, large dark eyes piercing as they looked at

Ravyn. "I wanted to give you a heads-up before you met with the new corporate folks."

Fingers twining tightly over the keyboard, lines creased Ravyn's forehead as she listened.

"Straight-shooting? They don't want nature-adventure or romance anymore. They don't want fiction pieces period."

Ravyn's eyebrows shot up in alarm. "I'm being fired?"

"No." Bev smiled. "They really like your style." Her mouth pressed into a thin line. "I worked hard to convince them that you do your best work in your current set-up but…" She looked at Ravyn again. "They're going to be asking for a big change from you."

Heart sinking, Ravyn kept her expression neutral. "They want me to commute."

"Not exactly." Bev bit her lip. "I can't say more, but go in prepared. I don't want us to lose you."

"Any idea why the change?" Her head hurt.

Bev groped for an explanation. "They didn't say. But they seemed pretty intent about –." She stopped, eyebrows pulling together.

Her breath short, head light, Ravyn blinked then prodded, "About what? Don't leave me with that."

Beverly hesitated. Her voice was low when she finally answered. "Ever heard of geo-mythology?"

Ravyn hadn't.

"Me either, but clearly they have. And somehow they think you're what they're looking for." She studied Ravyn through the webcam. "All I really know is it's going to be a big adjustment for you," she repeated. "But change, like they say, it opens up new horizons."

"Or obliterates treasured ones. I don't like commuting. Or working around other people."

Bev looked at her hands. "It's definitely more than an office commute."

Ravyn frowned and crossed her arms. "Meaning?"

"I'll say this." Bev's lips pursed momentarily. "It involves planes."

"Planes!" Pupils dilating, Ravyn leaned forward. "I don't fly!"

"I know." Her editor didn't meet Ravyn's eyes.

"I need to find another job."

"Hear them out first. And do me a favor." Bev smiled as she too leaned forward, her gaze once again holding Ravyn's own as she spoke in a near-whisper. "This is advice as a long-time friend. It could probably get me fired if I gave it as your boss."

Ravyn frowned.

"Meet your photographer first before making any decision." Raising her voice to normal levels again, she added, "Like you, he can get kind of bookish. Academic, if you know what I mean. I think you're going to like him. All of them up there really." She paused, as if waiting for Ravyn to respond. "Any questions?"

But the first bit had silenced Ravyn. As did the second. Herself? Academic? Anything but. She'd take fantasy over factual any day. Though, of course, it did have to have a good grounding in reality, like the story she'd just submitted last night drawing on research she'd been doing for a while about the Wood Wide Web.

Bev took the opportunity in Ravyn's silence to wish her well and sign off, ending the meeting.

It was only as she stared at the white blankness in front of her that Ravyn found the lurking question she wanted to ask. "Photographer?" she echoed to the empty screen.

Another more pressing issue supplanted this, however. Bev had said the new position involved airplanes.

Opening an internet tab, Ravyn started searching the web for job sites. She was scanning the fifth copy-editor position when she blinked, recollecting a minor detail from

Bev's conversation she'd not thought twice about at the time.

"All of them up where?"

Her only answer was a cat-smile. Curled in Ravyn's lap, paws kneading the chair cushion with eyes half-closed, Pyxi at least seemed certain all was right with the world.

"Maybe I'll wait for that email." Ravyn closed the laptop lid.

Eyes narrowed, faint lines of crowsfeet deepening, she stared at the closed computer for some minutes, one hand resting on it.

Finally, slowly, she lifted the lid again. "G. E. O," she said typing the term "geomythology" into Google.

A lot of links popped onto her screen.

" 'Legends of the earth,' " she read out loud and with unexpected interest. " 'Anthropology of landscape.' 'Tribal stories.' 'Pre-scientific cultures'?" She muttered rebelliously at that last description. "As if tribal societies didn't have science." Anyone who'd watched her mother work with plants only to later enjoy the results saw that right away. "Always ask permission of Nature," she'd told Ravyn countless times as a kid. "It's the way. Of Ifa. Minobimaatisiwin. All of those. And time-tested too." It was applied science. Knowledge from generations of observation. And kind of hard to replace once lost.

Still, interest piqued despite this, Ravyn continued scrolling through the listing of links, her posture straightening as she scanned the search page.

Klamath stories and the eruption that led to the creation of Crater Lake.

Ojibwe constellations and the annual floodings of spring.

Thunderbirds and teratorns.

Words like "antiquity" and "megaliths" started appearing in the link summaries, and she stopped for a moment, eyebrows rising. Clicking to the next page, she leaned forward. " 'Protecting the Future,' " she read. " 'Indigenous Prophecies as Geomythological Predictions.' "

With a glance down at Pyxi, she rubbed a finger under her cat's chin. "Intriguing possibilities there." Ravyn clicked the link, eyes narrowed the better to see the small font. " 'Our relationship to the land determines humanity's geologic fate.' "

She looked at Pyxi again. "Geologic fate?"

Pyxi continued to purr, watching Ravyn.

"Prophecies. Trees dying. Coasts flooding. Earth's axis shifting. Okay. Yeah. Big picture stuff alright." She skimmed the article silently, only breaking the peace with the concluding line. " 'It's not inevitable. We have a choice.' "

Ravyn stared unblinking at the screen, fingers aching to write.

It may have been many minutes she sat like that. Or only moments.

Forgetting her fiction no longer had a guaranteed audience through the magazine, Ravyn shut the laptop lid and grabbed her ideas notebook from the desk drawer instead, paper whispering as she leafed quickly through to a blank page.

A world in crisis. An Indigenous prophecy from time out of time. Would today's scientists recognize the warnings? It was going to take a dedicated geomythologist...and a stranger she had yet to meet.

Pyxi stood in Ravyn's lap and stretched carefully to keep her balance before wending her way up to the desk, laying across the top of the notebook. She placed a soft paw on the back of Ravyn's hand. Slanting green eyes blinked slowly, carefully following the words as they were scribbled across the page.

Chapter Three

Ice crystals spattered the hood of Ravyn's car, its engine dead in the storm. The woods crowded close and dark as winds buffeted their stalwart trunks leaving them caked with snow. "Fairy frogs," Ravyn quietly griped. Clutching the useless steering wheel, eyes closed, she pressed her forehead to the back of her hands. "Should of stayed home and written that story."

And she should have known better. No sane person simply followed the bidding of a stranger, new boss or no, into the depths of some of the most mysterious territory in Michigan's Upper Peninsula. It wasn't as if the signs hadn't tried to warn her...

By the time evening came the day of Bev's big announcement, the morning's chill had crept in and settled around the outside of Ravyn's home, gathering as an icy fog. It was as if the cold front sucked the very warmth from the land. Snow fell like a fine veil, obscuring the homes of even Ravyn's closest neighbors. The steady ringing of the buoy bell from down in the harbor was the only clue there were others beyond her doorstep. As evening wore on, the winter's fog remained, drawing close to her home like an animal seeking warmth.

Or like a protective presence, holding her safe in a misty world all its own.

Ravyn had spent the day running from her new job prospect by either furiously scribbling notes on her geomythology story or seeking career alternatives on the internet.

An hour before midnight, however, spent on her story ideas for now and exhausted from imagining herself in any number of new roles from copy-editor (she'd even sent in an application – and been congratulated on being applicant number four thousand and fifty-one) to video game storyteller (with a background so spotty she could only remember PacMan and Space Invaders), Ravyn bowed to her fate. The revised position at the magazine was clearly the only choice on the path of least resistance.

For now.

She checked her inbox, certain THE message, the one from corporate she'd been avoiding all day, had to have arrived by now.

It hadn't.

Maybe they'd changed their collective corporate mind and had decided to fire her. Ready to log off on that dismal thought, as if on cue her laptop pinged at 11:01 p.m.

A new message sat at the top of the list in her inbox. Bold type declared the sender as "Bianca Midé, CEO." The subject "New position with MegaLit, Inc."

Taking a deep breath, wondering how a mere click of the index finger on a mouse button could feel so dramatic, she opened the message.

For all the build-up, the text was rather anti-climatic.

"Ms. Shaunessy," it read. "We look forward to discussing your new position here at MegaLit tomorrow, 11 a.m., at our headquarters. Directions are below."

Bianca's signature listed "Geomythology, Ph.D." as one of many credentials. Beneath it, the directions began.

"As if I don't know where corporate offices are." Ravyn sniffed. It was clearly a barb, chastising her for not showing up at the morning's meeting.

But then she looked more closely. "You don't go north on 123 and – ," she began out loud. "That would take you – " Ravyn stopped, eyes widening. "Past the actual gates?" She quickly googled things just to confirm she wasn't misreading the directions.

She wasn't.

It didn't make any sense, but there it was. The Hidden Mountains. Forests of legend. Although her hometown nestled up against the base of their foothills, the mountains themselves were little more than distant shadowy forms. Looming on the horizon, they were known largely for casting darkness early across the evening landscape, a shadow that strengthened winter's icy grip.

Not knowing if there would be cell service that remote, Ravyn saved the rather complex directions to her travel phone – plugged in to charge for the commute – where she could access them offline. She went to sleep that night, comforter tucked beneath her chin, staring out the window, its panes frosted with the cozy warmth of a home tucked away from the chill world beyond.

The next morning, loaded with snacks for the trip in her beloved old Ford Escort, Ravyn tightened the wire that held the rearview mirror straight, checked the passenger door to make sure it would stay closed – given that it sometimes didn't – and pulled onto the main road for a ways before heading off into the more isolated countryside. Bare-limbed maples arched over the backwoods byway. The road was snowy from an early morning squall. Littered with branches tossed down by the gusting wind, it made the driving slow.

Slow enough to make the phone call she'd forgotten yesterday. Before she would inevitably lose signal.

Situating her phone carefully in its hands-free holder, she called Kaye, sipping the last of her green tea as the line rang.

"About time!" Kaye was indignant.

Ravyn filled her in.

A new position. Something about a photographer? And airplanes. Bev had warned her there would be airplanes. Oh yeah, and there was this meeting with the new boss in, you know (breath here to maintain a casual demeanor), the Hidden Mountains.

There was silence on the other end, one that held so long Ravyn craned her neck to see the phone, wondering if she still had service.

Then Kaye spoke slow and low. "I don't know anybody, I mean nooo...body" – Kaye dragged out the last word in a way that made Ravyn think uncomfortably of missing persons reports and vehicles abandoned deep in the woods – "who's been there before. Or at least has been there and lived to tell the tale."

"Thanks for the melodrama."

"You know the stories."

Ravyn did. And had been trying hard not to remember them.

"Think it's at that secret club place?" Kaye's voice sounded eager.

"I think – " Ravyn swallowed before continuing. "I think that's where the directions go to."

There was silence on the other end. Then Kaye added, "No civilization. Mile after mile of wilderness."

Ravyn was driving through that already. It seemed an interminable time since there had been another vehicle on the road.

"Rugged shorelines. Untamed waterfalls," Kaye continued. "Mythic beasts."

Ravyn cut in. "There aren't any mythic beasts." Her retort came out more forcefully than she'd intended.

Tires thudding over the rutted blacktop, winds off the lake buffeted Ravyn's car as she drove past a well used roadside turn-off, the last place to turn back and return to more civilized realms. Stern red and white signs forbid any stopping, standing or parking to enjoy Lake Superior's cliffside view.

"You know they've got those perimeter patrols," Kaye was saying.

Ravyn knew. Ignoring the dark clouds gathering at the rim of the horizon, she drove by the turn-off. The lake's slate blue waters, white-capped yet ice-free, reflected an incoming storm.

"Are they to keep us out?" Kaye dropped her voice. "Or to keep something in?"

"Those were just ghost stories. We were kids." But Ravyn felt a chill.

Kaye didn't respond.

"Hello?" Ravyn asked.

Only silence answered.

Bars at zero, she drew a deep breath and hung up on the dead signal.

More cliffside views and snowy woodlands rolled by mile after mile. Eyeing the clouds glowering through the trees lakeside, Ravyn eventually felt compelled to check the radio for weather alerts.

Nothing but static.

Slowing to take the next icy bend, a security gate abruptly emerged from the forest edge, bisecting the road ahead. A narrow and snow-covered lane disappeared into the woods beyond.

An elaborate sign proclaimed this the "Hidden Mountains Wilderness: A Secured Association" in elegant black lettering. What looked like a stone guardhouse stood to its side. A whirl of flurries blew from the forest, briefly obscuring the small building. When it cleared, a uniformed sentry was visible standing beside the place. He waited as she slowed then stopped at the gate.

Rolling down her window, there was an almost palpable presence to the air outside. Perhaps the feeling came from the sudden stillness of the wind. Or perhaps Kaye was right. The Mountains held old secrets. Apparitions. Bigfoot. Little folk. Even ghosts of the Huron who'd sought refuge in these hills generations ago.

Shoving such feelings aside as so much freaky imagination, Ravyn smiled at the guard.

Gray furred Kramer perched on his head, earflaps tied up, he did not return the greeting. If anything, his brows seemed to draw more tightly together. "Guest?" he asked curtly.

"Um," Ravyn stalled, not sure if she was. "Employee?"

"Badge?"

Ravyn wondered if multi-syllable sentences were against association regulations. "Uh, no. No badge."

Eyes narrowed he craned his neck to survey inside her car then began a slow pace around it.

"Well, I'm, uh, here to meet my new boss. At MegaLit?" Ravyn called out the window, not sure why she'd presented that information as a question rather than a statement. She fumbled with her phone to find the email Bianca had sent. It took until the guard had circumnavigated the full perimeter of her vehicle to remember she didn't have service.

"ID."

Assuming he meant some id from her, she gave him her driver's license.

Studying it for what seemed several minutes, he handed it back to her then returned to the guardhouse. The gate remained closed. Through the building's small window, he indicated she should wait as he lifted a handset.

Ravyn couldn't hear him, but his lips seemed to move in complete sentences. Brief but definitely more than mono-syllabic.

Suddenly, with a clang followed by a drawn out creak as if all the Celtic banshees were trapped inside, the black wrought iron gate slid slowly across the drive. Leaving a drag line in the snowy gravel, it disappeared into the woods alongside the rest of the fence.

Ravyn drove in, waving slightly without looking to see if the guard returned the gesture.

The sky darkened. But the forest didn't change perceptibly.

The sudden appearance of old-fashioned wood signage was a little startling. Exquisite yet obscure calligraphy and cracked paint lent the impression the signs had been there for some time as did the moss nestled snugly into worn pits and crumbling edges. Ravyn couldn't decipher the words. It was hard to tell if her difficulty stemmed from it being written in such a faded and fancy form of calligraphy or, her imagination working overtime, if it was written in an entirely different alphabet than English.

"Get a grip," she muttered.

A couple narrow, unplowed sideroads no wider than two-tracks branched off from the main graveled lane, winding quickly into the forest. Ravyn thumbed her phone for the directions she'd saved, the coverage bars at zero.

She pretended to ignore this last observation as well as the sudden flutter in her stomach. Cut off from the outside world – lots of people thought that was a good thing. As long as there were no flat tires or sudden appearances of scary beasts, it would all be okay. Plump snowflakes brushed against her windshield, blowing off in a gust of wind.

Yeah, and not getting lost in a sudden snowstorm would be good too.

"Five point two miles then take a right. I can handle that." Re-setting the old-fashioned rollover trip odometer, she also switched on the headlights. Though nearing eleven in the morning, the lowering sky made it feel like twilight.

The road, barely more than a one-laner, twisted left then right so frequently she wasn't able to drive over thirty. She checked the clock again – she wasn't late yet. Despite the short distance Ravyn had traveled since she'd passed through the gate, it felt like an hour had passed.

Three point seven miles.

The snow began to fall heavy enough to require top speed on the wipers. They sliced efficiently across the windshield, clearing a line of sight through the blanket of white powder.

Four point zero.

Four point two.

Her right turn arrived. The road, its freshly fallen snow unmarred by recent tracks, was even narrower than the main one.

Thumbing her phone to scroll through the directions, she found there was another mile to go before she reached the driveway of her destination. Whether it was on the left or the right, they didn't say. Presumably there would only be one choice. The directions had nothing more to reveal after that.

About half a mile in, the car jerked convulsively. Faltered. Convulsed again. Then stopped. The wheels continued to roll silently with momentum for several seconds before she thought to steer to the side of the narrow road.

Trying to start the car, it caught, sputtered and died again.

"Fairy frogs!" Ravyn cried out and tried a second time, pumping the accelerator.

No response other than the momentary brightening of dashboard lights.

Her gas gauge said there was over a three-quarters tank, just as much as she'd started the day with.

That was the giveaway.

Ravyn flicked the gauge with her finger. The needle dropped to the bottom of the red. The gauge worked fine. Except when it didn't. It was at its most temperamental in cold weather, something she stupidly hadn't thought of when she set out earlier.

Dropping her head against the headrest, Ravyn idly picked up her phone even as she knew there were no bars to speak of. But she had to check just to be sure.

Zero.

Unreasonable as it may have been, Ravyn turned the key in the ignition again.

The engine groaned. And stalled.

On the next stubborn try, there was nothing at all. Not even a faint flicker from the lights on the dash.

The wind outside clawed at the driver's window, snow shrouding the windshield. A chill crept into the little car.

Melting a circle with her thumb in the window's coalescing frost, she looked out at the snow swirling densely through the encroaching woods just beyond the glass.

As the tip of her nose grew cold, Ravyn became certain of one thing – she couldn't just sit in the car forever, slowly cooling down in her dress coat and boots. The silk blouse that this morning had felt so luxurious as she'd slipped it on was beginning to feel like an icy sheath. And newsflash: nylons did very little to keep out the cold.

It's not like she couldn't get out and walk. A half-mile wasn't a marathon. Incentivized by the cold, it would take no more than ten minutes. Tops.

Chapter Four

Stifling a demoralizing sigh, Ravyn pushed open the car door and stepped outside. Wind struck her in the face, flattening her skirt against her legs as she pulled a light-weight coat close. Pressing against the wind to reach the trunk, she rummaged there through the detritus of summer road trips. A musty-smelling swimsuit she'd never brought in to dry. A bottle of bug spray as useless to her now as it had been in the heat of summer. Finally she found the emergency winter duffle bag packed last month. A quick slam of the trunk and she hustled back into the driver's seat, shutting out the wind, the thin shield of window glass dulling its roar.

Halfway through unzipping the duffle, Ravyn stopped, peering more closely into the woods, certain she'd seen a shadow in that snow-ridden forest beyond. But nothing materialized. Eyes on the trees, she slowly unfastened the bag, the quietly harsh ripping sound of the zipper like that of fabric tearing open to another world.

Sweater. Jeans. Warm boots and a down parka. With these plus several granola bars and a small, frozen package of emergency water she'd had the foresight to pack, she could easily venture that last half mile. After a change swift and smooth enough for Superman to envy, Ravyn neatly stuffed her work clothes into the bag, remembering her heels at the last minute, and pushed the door open one last time.

The wind bit. Hard. The snow fell even more thickly. Duffle bag slung over her shoulder, Ravyn plunged down the empty road which, though snow-covered, seemed easy enough to follow. When a half-mile later she reached the point where the directions had left off, two driveways branched perpendicular to the road's end forming a perfect T. Too late Ravyn remembered she'd left her cell phone in the pocket of her dress coat back in the car. Doubting further guidance could be found there anyway, she studied the drives for a clue.

Neither one was wider than a snowmobile trail.

Neither had a special sign or an address number.

One had not so much as a rabbit's track to blemish the freshness of the snow. The drive to the left, however, held a faint set of tracks, much blown over but apparent nonetheless. They were large. And more importantly, human-shaped.

Ravyn set out to follow them.

At first the tracks wound faithfully with the drive, and Ravyn trotted along happy in the certainty that help and warmth were ahead, her steps light despite the continually mounting snow and frigid wind.

The further she walked, however, the fiercer the storm became. Flurries turned into wind-blasted precipitation. It drowned the crunch of her boots on the snow. Visibility dropped, her vision narrowing until all the world seemed to exist as a bleary white tunnel. Ravyn could only follow one swiftly vanishing footprint after the other, shoving back the growing alarm she felt.

The wind shifted briefly. Calm descended. The snow still fell, but Ravyn could see again. The tracks she followed, increasingly obscured by the storm, wound into more trees ahead. But the drive itself was no longer visible. It wasn't simply that it had been snowed over. It just wasn't there. The trees grew wild as they do in a forest with neither a road nor a drive of any kind forged between them. Several hundred thousand untamed acres of the Hidden Mountains lay before her.

Several hundred thousand acres of desolation.

The idea of wilderness with all its untamed beauty never seemed to deserve its desolate reputation before. But here. Now. She understood.

With her trail behind hardly visible and with the surety that ahead someone had recently trekked through, it seemed unwise to turn back.

Plunging further into the forest, massive trunks of sugar maple rose around her. The freezing gale howled overhead, and the storm suffocated the light.

Lumbering one frozen foot in front of the other, her legs no longer felt as if they belonged to her but were merely mechanical stilts, borrowed for the sole purpose of propelling her through the snow.

Time wore on. Interminably.

Slowly...vaguely...she came to a dread understanding: the trail of tracks she'd been following, the lifeline on which she relied, had faded. Wholly and completely. Lost to the rushing of the wind.

Praying she'd strayed from the faint prints only moments ago she stumbled back trying to retrace her steps, but the wind was a powerful scour.

There was nothing.

Panic lurched Ravyn forward toward a hemlock copse ahead. Beneath the conifers, branches created a shelter from much of the storm. The wind still clawed its way around the trunks, whistling as it blew though ultimately thwarted by the protective grove.

The loneliness of things crept into her bones, settling there. It was a loneliness she'd known only once before when, just seven years old, she'd wandered off. Though she didn't remember much, there were certain details she'd never forget. A lake of rough waters. Pines loomed where she'd been certain their picnic table was supposed to be. The wind howled, its chill like beastly fingers reaching for her as the summer skies darkened just before the storm fell. That the world could feel so empty, so fierce, had never occurred to her little-girl mind. She'd torn fingernails digging into an old animal burrow trying to escape the terror of it.

Taken back to that time, even now as a grown woman Ravyn closed her eyes as she'd done years ago, whispering nonsense and nursery rhymes as a bulwark against the cold and windswept dark.

Back then when they'd found her the next morning she was sitting in a patch of sunshine and wintergreen, leaves in her mussy braids, talking to the berries. Perversely, she hadn't wanted to leave.

Separation fed desolation. Loneliness was one thing. Solitude another.

Eyes opening, she pressed her palm to the trunk of a giant hemlock, noting the sapsucker holes on its trunk, the pileated burrow in an old yellow birch nearby, the tiny tight buds of a maple by its side already preparing for spring. Slowly, muscle by muscle, she leaned into the stout and steadfast tree, cheek coming to rest against its rough bark.

Pulling out one of the granola bars stashed in her coat pockets, hungry as she was her stomach rebelled at first. And for a moment, she did too. She'd come out here for a simple interview with new bosses. Not to embark on a death-defying quest, wandering the wilderness with only her winter-survival bag on which to rely. A bag she'd packed with the perfectly sensible intent of staying warm while she waited in the vehicle for help she'd always assumed would come in the event of car troubles.

None of this had been on MegaLit's trip itinerary.

The hemlock branches, lacy green against the whitely blowing snow, suddenly lifted in the wind. Through the gap in the grove's greenery, a tall, dark silhouette was barely visible as it moved swiftly through the storm, disappearing behind tall trunks of trees just beyond the curtain of swirling snow.

Ravyn forgot her granola bar, dropping it and its wrapper on the snowdrifts to reel forward into the storm.

The dark shape was very large. Surely human. Bears were hibernating. Moose didn't walk upright. There was nothing else it could resemble.

She called out.

The figure stilled, seeming to listen, but then moved quickly away again.

Ravyn pitched into the storm, the wind tearing at her coat, her hair, despite the deep forest all around. The figure remained ahead, moving quickly yet always visible, even pausing on occasion as if waiting for her to catch up. During these pauses, Ravyn came almost near enough to see who it was she was following. But always the silhouette moved on before she could get a clear view. And, whoever her mystery hero, he was either too far to hear her calls. Or was intentionally not answering them.

She wasn't sure how long she followed the figure. It could have been ten minutes. It seemed like hours. Her face felt as if it would fall off were she to touch it. Cold pierced her gloves. Fingers numb, she pulled her arms into her parka, hands stuffed under armpits to keep them warm, bracing herself against the nearly horizontal storm winds.

An abrupt gale blasted into her face before it shifted dramatically as if blowing from the ground up, tossing snow into the air. Ahead and to her left, the dim form disappeared completely into a pallid blur. Ravyn halted where she was, curling into a ball against a tree she wasn't able to see as the world became nothing more than a gusting of white.

When the squall cleared, her guide was no longer visible. All tracks had been whisked away by the winds.

Ravyn kicked at the snow, sending up no more than a diminutive puff. Leaning against the nearest tree, too exhausted to care what kind it was, she slid down its trunk, collapsing in the snow. She knew better than to close her eyes, for sleep would surely find her. Her granola bars were gone, the emergency water pack as useless as it was frozen. Having no matches, no flares, only her silk shirt in the duffle for added warmth, there seemed nothing else to do but watch the snowflakes as they fell like a heavy, white velvet curtain. Or more like it, her shroud.

It took her a bit to notice, but there was a familiar smell percolating through the woods. Giving an idle sniff, she suddenly straightened in recognition.

Woodsmoke, filtering through the storm. Its persistence was curious.

Pushing against the tree trunk to get to her feet, Ravyn faceplanted in a snowdrift. She pushed to her feet again. Face icy, white flakes clinging to her eyelashes, she peered through the snow and trees.

Ahead the warm glow of golden lights glimmered from an enormous stone and log chalet. Like a glamorous lodge for Northwoods

Barbie, it nestled among a forest of ancient pine, its walls more window than wood. Smoke curled out of its three stone chimneys. In one wing, golden lights on a tall, plump Christmas tree twinkled through frosted windowpanes. Only the multiple vehicles parked in the driveway dulled the fairy tale effect.

Warmth.

Food.

Shelter.

Ravyn started eagerly forward, then stopped, remembering the person who had led her here. Maybe this was his home. Or maybe he was lost as much as she. The last snow squall could have hidden the house from him too.

"Hello?" she called into the wind. But the word was torn from her mouth, dispersed like so many tiny snowflakes into the vastness of the storm. She tried being louder, hoping volume alone could overcome the sheer force of the wind. "Hello! There's a house over here!"

Nothing.

Inside, though, there would be help. The added impetus pushed her tired legs through the snow toward the house, if such a term could be used to describe a place so grand.

In the drive, drifts lapped over the hoods of neatly parked vehicles, most a sleek and shiny black. Ravyn followed a path - recently shoveled but already filling in with snow - as it curved from the vehicles to an arched portico. She was met there by an imposing double wooden door and gold door knockers, stately even in their turtle form. She gripped one tight, drew a deep breath and knocked, clumsily, hands stiff with the cold.

Minutes seemed to pass. She leaned against the doorjamb.

Just as she labored to raise her hand and knock again, one of the doors opened.

On the other side stood a skinny young woman, her good bone structure emphasized by the bun in which she'd drawn back her blonde hair. Faint wisps escaped around her face. She was dressed formally. White shirt, bow tie and black feminine slacks with stiletto heels. Her ready smile froze when she saw Ravyn. Then her eyes widened. "Don't you look like the abominable snowman," she said by way of greeting. "Come in and get warmed up."

Weakly stomping the snow from her boots, Ravyn followed mutely, blinking at the sudden emergence into warmth and quiet. Fire crackled in a nearby fireplace. A round throw rug covered the floor's flagstone tiles. The woman led her to a pair of graceful chairs, angled side by side facing the fire, each with rich burgundy cushions.

"Let me take your things." She held out her hand for Ravyn's coat. "I'll tell Ms. Bianca you're here. You're Ravyn Shaunessy, right? We were getting worried." She looked closely at Ravyn. "You alright?"

Snow fell from Ravyn's shoulders to the floor, melting quickly into pools of water. She nodded again, too tired to be surprised at having arrived, somehow, at the very destination she'd been striving for. Fingers stiff, she struggled with the jacket zipper, eventually wresting herself out of the parka. It was a relief to settle into a comfortable chair with the warmth of the fire on her face.

The woman turned to go but hesitated. "You sure you're okay?"

Ravyn managed a weak smile which worked to reassure them both.

"Just sit here," the woman said briskly. "I'll have someone bring you hot tea. Or maybe cocoa?"

Ravyn pushed on another small smile as she sat heavily in the chair nearest the fire. Hot anything would do. She closed her eyes a moment then sat upright, eyes wide. "Wait!" she blurted. "There's somebody still out there." But her eyelids were heavier than she ever remembered. She sank back into the chair. "I think he may need help."

"Oh." Hand covering her mouth, gaze darting about as if looking for him in that very room, the woman embellished her original comment, "Oh. Oh, my." Apparently having nothing more revelatory to say, she left immediately.

The next few minutes Ravyn made a great effort to remain alert as the steady warmth of the fire worked its magic. There were the sounds of hurried footsteps scuffling on the stone floor. A small multitude of people appeared with questions for Ravyn. Where? Who? How long ago? She answered as best she could, pushing against the heavy weight of impending sleep.

"She's tired out, Bianca." A man's voice drifted idly through Ravyn's half-awake state.

A woman's voice answered. "No wonder. Let her rest, poor thing."

"Think the trackers will find someone?"

"Or something," another man, his voice familiar yet not, quietly said. "This storm, with it coming I should have met her at the gate."

Vaguely wondering at his trace accent – French, maybe Spanish? – eyes too leaden to open, Ravyn let herself fall heavily into that gray fog of sleep.

hapter Five

Echoes of distant laughter woke Ravyn.

Brilliant white sunshine blinded her at first, and she held up a hand to ward off the light, wincing, cheeks stiff. Touching them lightly, ointment of some sort stuck to her fingertips smelling a little like bacon and a lot like onion.

Ravyn spread the fingers that held back the sun, allowing a bit of the bright light to stream through, eyes adjusting before she lowered her hand completely. Beyond the paned floor-to-ceiling window, snow still fell, now light and lazy, despite the sunshine and largely blue skies. Magnificent hardwoods and pines crowded close, their branches heavy with snow from the storm.

Someone had pulled a warm blanket over her, curled up as she was in the armchair. A tentative stretch proved all was in working order. She could feel her toes. Each finger was accounted for.

Reveling in the warmth now that she was fully conscious, Ravyn pulled the blanket to her chin, not yet wanting to stir and get on with things. The fire continued to crackle in the fireplace, flames hypnotic. The cream-colored walls drew close in a friendly, comforting sort of way.

Ravyn straightened, willing her drooping eyelids open, and blinked rapidly. Her vision blurry at first, it took a minute for several tapestries that hung nearby to come into focus. Threads of silver and gold caught the daylight. One of the tapestries had been woven as a beautiful but fairly ordinary orchard scene of two people sitting beneath an apple tree. In the other, though, the same-colored threads shimmered as part of a rope from which a couple in a hand basket descended through a hole in the starry sky.

Vaguely, Ravyn wondered if she might still be dreaming.

"Do you need anything, miss?"

Jerking her head at the man's voice, Ravyn wrenched a muscle in her neck. Pressing her lips to keep from crying out, she managed a "No, thank-you" with a tight smile.

His demeanor was nearly as stiff as his starched butler's suit, but his voice was kind. A polite and solicitous exchange of words and Ravyn discovered her 11 a.m. meeting was still on even though greatly delayed. Their boss was ready when she was. And people were actually waiting on her arrival somewhere in a room down a maze of halls that, so the butler explained, branched off from the cozy alcove in which she'd hoped to remain for a while longer yet.

Face flushing, Ravyn gathered the blanket preparatory to folding it. Her purse, open, dropped from its plush depths, scattering a variety of items on the floor at her feet. She snatched at her wallet, vaguely fumbling at everything else, dropping smaller articles almost as quickly as she picked up others.

The butler handed her a silver tube of lipstick.

Mumbling her thanks, Ravyn tucked snow-dampened hair behind her ear and asked, "Is there a restroom or something?" Her voice remained soft.

"Of course." He smiled, pointing down the same hallway he'd previously indicated as leading to Bianca's office. "First door you come to. And I can take that for you." He pointed to the rumpled blanket in her arms.

Duffle bag clutched to her chest, Ravyn hurried along, curious about the staircase wending off from the hall. Treads edged with gold trim. Banisters in gold relief. It all curved in a Fibonacci pattern to areas made the more

mysterious by their apparently remote seques-
tration.

At the first door, Ravyn paused. A keypad
was affixed to the wall next to the closed door.
The butler (if that really was what he was –
she'd never met a butler before) hadn't said
anything about needing a passcode, of all
things, to use the bathroom. She tentatively
leaned a shoulder against the door. It opened a
little. Palm flat against the wood paneling, she
pushed through more confidently.

The first room, for there were several
behind the door, was a sitting room with two
winged armchairs and a chaise lounge. An
unobtrusive refrigerator was recessed into the
wall while a kitchenette, complete with
multiple and well-stocked storage shelves,
opened off the sitting room. The third room, a
private bathroom, also contained a shower. No
windows were visible. Ravyn peeked inside
one of the many cabinets built into the sitting
room walls. It contained a variety of board

games. A second held medical supplies and large jugs of water.

"Prepping for World War III, are we?" she muttered, shutting and locking the main door of the restroom before opening her bag. "Or collapse, maybe."

A quick glance in the mirror told her everything she suspected already, and she set to work gently dabbing the ointment off her flushed and wind-burned cheeks, ignoring the wild state of her hair for the moment.

Whisking out of the sweater and jeans, Ravyn slipped back into her baby blue silk blouse and the swishy knee-length skirt to match. Her nylons had a run in them which held her up some minutes more before she decided to bareleg it. Then a quick slip on of the slingbacks, a hasty brushing, mussing, then smoothing of her black curls, a swift application of pearl pink lipstick, and she was out the door.

There was a difficult balance to strike between keeping her breath and hustling to meet her new boss, heels thudding dully like some sort of erratic drumbeat on the hallway's Persian-esque carpet. Just as the rhythm settled into a steady pattern, an invisible door hidden seamlessly into the wall opened, and Ravyn stumbled. A dark-haired woman with glasses, eyes widening, quickly shut the door again leaving Ravyn alone in the hall once more.

But she'd caught a glimpse inside the room. An art gallery. With a secret door. Evidently housing valuable art indeed.

Light from another open doorway spilled onto the burgundy carpet at the end of the hallway. Last room on the right, the butler guy had said. And so it was.

Hesitating in the doorway, the first thing Ravyn noticed was a tall man, his unruly dark hair secured in a shoulder-length ponytail. In jeans and a navy flannel shirt, sleeves rolled to three-quarters, he stood relaxed but with good bearing, his back to the room, apparently intent on the view outside the large cathedral window.

And no wonder. Craggy cliffs curved outward, stretching along the shore of the lake, its horizon limitless as it glistened under the sun. White-capped waves crashed against the gray cliff base far below. Several seagulls, either intent on overwintering or late to the migration trip that year, rode the wind currents. Even as expert fliers a couple of the birds were blown nearer the cliffs, both veering sharply at the last moment.

The office was not lit like a typical office. With no visible sources of light other than the window, the room – or rather suite of rooms – was suffused with a warm glow. A large executive desk sat at the back of the main room situated to face the window that looked out on the lake. Sitting at the desk was a striking woman, black hair gracefully swept back into a French twist. She held a paper in one hand but was looking through several others on her glass-top desk.

The wall behind her was taken up with oblong tapestries five or six feet tall, maybe three or so feet wide. Their size and similarity in the colored threads hinted they were a set. The forest scene depicted across the tapestry panels confirmed it. Towering conifers and deciduous trees were present on all. Various woodland critters hid in their branches, but a wolf, what looked to be a Sasquatch figure, and other animals like a turtle and an eagle each held a place of significance in panels of their own. The same silver and gold threads Ravyn had observed in the tapestries back in the fireplace foyer were used in these as well. Gold for the sunlight in the leftmost depictions. Silver for the moon and starlight on the rightmost. She counted seven in all.

In an adjoining anteroom, a short, trim man was hanging a framed photograph as part of what looked to be a collection of photographs. Light glinted off the smooth skin of his bald head hinting at recessed ceiling fixtures.

The woman looked up from her papers, smiling when she saw Ravyn hovering in the doorway. She stood to skirt around her desk, hand extended. "So good to see you feeling better." Her smiled broadened. "Truly, it's a pleasure to meet you. I'm a big fan. Come, Damien, Oliver," she said with as kindly a commanding tone as Ravyn had ever heard. "Meet our new writer." She led Ravyn to a cluster of chairs in front of a stone fireplace. Warm golden flames licked the grate.

"New writer" might be stretching it. As far as Ravyn was concerned, this was an interview in which she would judge whether or not to accept this new position. She perched on the chair, elbow on an armrest. Its cushions were just comfortable enough in which to relax, but not so soft a person would sink in deep, fighting the urge to nap. Especially after a recent blizzard's hike.

At Bianca's summons, the man in the anteroom had put the framed photo on the floor, leaning it against the wall, and made his way over quickly. This was Oliver, Ravyn learned. Making Damien the man at the window, his gaze still fixed on the distant horizon. Silence like a stratus cloud settled on the coalescing group as they waited for him to join the circle.

Ravyn cleared her throat, the sound louder than she intended. She smiled apologetically and, shifting in the seat, ventured into conversation. "Is he doing alright?" she asked. At their blank looks, she amended. "The man in the storm. The one who led me here?"

Bianca smiled tentatively. "He's, um...last reports were...he's doing fine."

"Could I see him?" Ravyn asked on impulse. "Before I leave, I mean. To thank him for – "

"I'm afraid that's not possible." Bianca's curt interruption belied the easygoing friendliness in her persistent smile. "But I'm sure he's aware."

Walking so softly Ravyn hadn't heard him, Damien joined the circle, settling in the chair next to her. He exchanged a look with Bianca as he did so.

Ravyn's own smile was half-hearted. She glanced at Damien who was studying his palms as he leaned forward, elbows on knees. A lock of dark hair fell across his forehead, and he absently pushed it behind his ear. Returning her gaze to Bianca, "Okay" was all she could think to say.

"Damien," he said as he reached a hand toward her. "Damien Le Sauvage."

Starting a little, her fingers lightly taking his, Ravyn gave Damien a tentative handshake.

His own was firm, but gentle. "And you must be Ravyn." There was a delightful hint of an accent in those words. French, judging by his last name.

"Yep. Uh-huh," she said, face flushing. "Nice to meet you."

"*Enchanté*," he said.

Their eyes only met for a moment, but Ravyn caught a sort of spark or glimmer in his. Was it humor? Arrogance? It surely couldn't be interest. Her blush deepened at the thought.

"So," Bianca began brightly. "Shall we?"

Chapter Six

The lights dimmed – to Ravyn's relief. A panel opened in the wall above the fireplace, revealing a multimedia screen where a MegaLit logo held the center. As if it were a megalith in and of itself, the logo resembled a book in an ancient forest, each of its two open pages like elements of stone from which young saplings sprouted. A scattering of stars arced overhead.

It was most unusual.

Bianca crooked an index finger to her left. "Jeff?" A man in a formal black suit emerged from deep shadows Ravyn hadn't realized were there. "Bring the refreshments, if you please. Thank-you."

Jeff nodded and disappeared only to re-emerge moments later with a silver cart loaded with various carafes, pastries and fruit. Ravyn hadn't realized how hungry she was.

The food made its way around the small circle. "Our apologies for the extensive drive," Bianca said. "It was necessary, as you'll see." She glanced at Damien. "No doubt sometime Damien will share with you the importance of having a safe house to come to. Sometimes there can be..." She paused, apparently searching for the right words. "Unpleasant residual business after returning home from an assignment."

Frowning, Ravyn tilted her head. Before she could formulate a coherent follow-up question, however, Bianca continued with a reassuring smile, "But today we're here to talk about your stories and your revised position." She took a small sip of juice. "Our job," Bianca offered, "is to use our art to protect those places that have a particularly sacred significance to the world."

Intriguing. Ravyn made a mental note.

On the screen in front of them, a slideshow of artistic renditions began. The Nazca geo-glyphs. The Jackson Hole Medicine Wheel. "Art generates protection. In various ways." Bianca paused, looking at Ravyn as if to make sure she was paying close attention.

Wishing she'd remembered the notebook and pen she'd left in her duffle, Ravyn nodded. Art got the word out about a place. And the more people knew, the more they cared. Got it.

"Then there's closer to home." An underwater photo spread across the screen. "We haven't done a deepwater site before, but this one's special. A stone circle ten thousand years old, plus or minus. And near Mackinac Island."

Brows pulling together, Ravyn tried to discern what she was supposed to see in the green-lit image of fuzzily moss covered rocks on a sandy lake bottom. It took some moments but when the broken shape of a definite circle suddenly popped into visibility it was difficult to un-see.

"There are other circles," Bianca began, but after a glance at Damien, she instead changed the topic with the slide. "Most of our sites are easier to access though. Like the Grand Island – Bay de Noc trail. Centuries old, millennia maybe, the energy there's very interesting."

As a world map slowly filled the screen, she smiled at Ravyn. "Only a handful of… publishers…like ours, do what we do. We each have responsibility for different regions. MegaLit? We're responsible for Europe and Turtle Island…" Bianca stopped. "North America, that is. Sometimes we get a call to help out elsewhere."

Things got that crazy in the sacred sites protection game? Ravyn's eyebrows raised skeptically before she remembered her income depended on remaining employed with MegaLit. At least until she could find another employer. If that was the route she chose anyway, after this interview.

"Your job..." Bianca continued slowly as the screen doors hummed shut behind her. The lighting returned to its warm glow. "Your job is to write narratives about unusual activity at these sacred places."

Straightening, Ravyn asked, "By narratives, you mean I'll still be able to write my stories?" That was some good news. She was no reporter. Ravyn daintily picked up a raspberry-filled pastry.

"Mmmm." Bianca hesitated. "A little yes, a little no. Write stories, yes. But they have to be true. Names can be changed, people not essential to the happenings can be fictionalized. But the phenomena described have to be real."

"I'm afraid fiction is all I really know how to do. Reality isn't exactly my forte." Ravyn suppressed an uneasy giggle. "I'm not sure how great I'd be at accurately recording something, even using a story-format."

Her original resistance to the new position mounted. Nonfiction was storytelling, sure, but a dry form of it. Deeper truths were often ignored with nonfiction, in favor of a presentation of facts arrayed in synchronous precision. But the world in all its swirling chaos didn't work that way. Not as she saw it anyway. Fiction got to the heart of things in a much clearer way.

Ravyn finished her pastry more quickly than she meant to.

Oliver looked at her, giving a brilliant smile. "You're the perfect fit, actually. We've been looking for some time." He glanced at Damien.

Damien's face reddened, and Oliver dropped his gaze.

Swiftly interjecting, Bianca continued. Her tone clearly implied she was relaying a major benefit of the position. "Your first assignment would be in France."

"France?" Bev had been right about the planes. "Now that's something – that's something I need to –." Ravyn came to a halt, realizing she didn't quite have the courage to confront her new boss on this point of contention.

Damien caught her attention, though, giving her a soft, nearly imperceptible smile.

"Um," Ravyn said again, drawing a deep breath. This had to be said. She began slowly, "If it involves travel...full disclosure, I'm not really a big traveler. Kind of the opposite actually."

"Bev told me you'd say that." Bianca's eyes softened. "You ever flown before?"

Mute, Ravyn shook her head, certain she didn't like where this was heading. Besides, "I don't even speak French," she said, as if that clinched things.

Bianca inclined her head across the half-circle. "You and Damien will be partners, meaning you'll both travel together. And his first language is French, so you'll be fine."

The pulse in Ravyn's throat made it difficult to get her words out. "Damien will be there?" Her voice came out higher than she intended. She coughed delicately. "I mean, I won't be going alone?"

Everyone shook their heads.

"And, Damien…" Ravyn turned to look at him but found it more comfortable to talk to her hands. "You're, ah…" She thought of what Bev had said about waiting to meet the photographer. "You take photos?"

He nodded. "The writing's your thing." He too dropped his gaze, studying his palms. "I just take the photos to go with it."

His accent made the English words seem almost magic in and of themselves. Bev made a lot more sense now.

"And what's, ah...what's in France?" Ravyn addressed this question to Bianca.

"Glad you asked." On cue, the screen doors slid open again. Flashing through a couple slides, Bianca stopped at one of a large table-top dolmen in a small copse of hardwoods. "La Roche aux Fées."

"Rock of the Fairies," Damien quietly translated for her.

Ravyn worked to keep her attention on what Bianca was saying.

"You may have heard of it from your research?"

True. There were a number of places with similar names she'd come across when researching plots and settings for those plots. Like fairy forts in general. Or specific sites such as Giant's Ring. But she didn't recall this one in particular.

Turns out, it was old. Five thousand years of old making it Neolithic like so many dolmens and stone circles in Europe were. Built with multiple stones, it was forty feet in length – what many considered the largest such structure in the world. "There seems to be a convergence. The state of the world. The coming fullness of the lunar cycle." Bianca fixed her eyes on Ravyn. "Reports are...the fairies have returned."

"Fairies." It felt like a test. Ravyn dropped Bianca's gaze. But, brows drawing together, she looked up at her again. "You don't mean fairy fairies." Once it was said aloud, Ravyn realized how silly it sounded. She forced a laugh. "I mean, of course you don't. Sorry."

But Bianca only shrugged. Glancing at her watch, she moved to perch on the edge of her chair. "These are reports only. And that's where you two come in. I'm sending you for the Winter Solstice. Jeff has the details." With that, she rose, skirting the outside of the circle. "If you'll excuse me, I see I'm late for another meeting." But she paused as she passed Ravyn, resting a hand lightly on her shoulder. "I know you don't like travel," she said. "And planes even less. Call this a trial run. See how it goes." She squeezed Ravyn's shoulder lightly before walking away. "It means everything to have you on the team. Jeff?"

Oliver trailed after Bianca.

Ravyn was left staring blankly at the vacated chairs, wondering what had just happened. They weren't seriously paying her to go to France and investigate reports of little flying people?

"Pretty unbelievable, eh?"

Starting at the sound of Damien's voice, Ravyn knocked her pastry napkin to the floor, quickly covering it with her foot before he noticed. "So you've been in the U.P. long enough to pick up the whole Yooper accent thing...eh?" She'd meant it, even the mimicked "eh" (pronounced almost like "hay" with a little less emphasis on the "h") as a flippant quip to distract from her first faux pas, but it all fell flat and he only gave her a strange look.

Clearing her throat, Ravyn folded her hands in her lap, thumbs tapping against each other. Now that she thought of it, maybe the conversational tic was part of the French language too. Which would explain its histor-ically entrenched prevalence in the Upper Peninsula, what with it once being part of New France. And later even the province of Québec. From the 1600s (some might say the 1500s) until 1783. Not that she was about to attempt an extemporaneous exposition on all this or anything. Admittedly, though, she did have to press her lips tight to keep the words from popping out.

Thinking a distraction in order, Ravyn belatedly remembered the original trajectory of Damien's comment.

Bringing her hazel eyes to meet his dark gray ones, hoping to recover at least some dignity despite herself, she protested, "Fairies don't exist." It had to be that all this talk of fairies and such in the interview was some sort of test, laying the bait to see how gullible she was. "The only place you'll find such creatures is in stories. It's called fantasy for a reason, you know."

"Could it be that stories, they're one way the unseen world makes itself known to us?"

Choosing to ignore this suggestion, Ravyn shifted focus. "This job – what do we do?" Without giving him time to answer, she held up a hand. "Don't tell me. Investigate ley lines? Leprechauns?"

"Leprechauns. If they warrant it."

"Then what?"

"Your story and my photos, we publish those together. Then they're put in the Gallery."

"Gallery?"

Smiling, he said, "More on that later."

Jeff returned, a sheaf of papers in hand which he offered to Ravyn.

As Ravyn took the folder, Damien rose and moved back to the window, looking out again at the lake, arms folded. A strip of braided leather was tied loosely around his wrist. Four small beads, yellow, red, black, and white, hung from it.

Turning her attention to the file, Ravyn riffled through the papers. Application for a passport. A rather concerning liability waiver for work-related risks. Travel tips. Her salary contract. This last caught and held Ravyn's attention. "These figures must be wrong."

"The salary?"

"Yeah."

Damien cleared his throat. "They pay well. Very well."

"This well?"

He nodded.

Tapping the papers against her palm, Ravyn paced over to the window. Just beyond the glass, the wind-whipped lake continued to dash fiercely against the dark gray cliffs. In the distance, sunlight caught the foaming froth of white-capped swells. "I hate travel."

"There are compensations."

She turned her back to the window, facing him. "Have *you* ever investigated reports of fairies before?"

"M-hm."

"Pixies?" She smirked.

"More than once."

Ravyn folded her arms. "What about parallel universes? Interdimensional shifts?" Her eyebrow hooked skeptically.

"Yes."

"Please don't say Bigfoot."

"Alright, then. I won't." But his smile told her all she didn't want to know.

Eyes narrowing, she asked, "And has any of it ever turned out to be real?"

Damien pushed away from the wall. Hands behind his back, he tilted his head. "I'm not going to answer that."

"Why not?"

"If I say yes, you won't believe me." He moved toward the door. Ravyn followed. "If I say no, this will seem like wasted time. It's up to you to decide."

"Would you recommend the job?"

"Absolutely."

"Why?"

"Come to France. Decide what you think when we get back." Damien smiled. "You might be surprised."

She could feel the pulse in her neck throbbing, as it was wont to do at times like these. "I've never flown."

"MegaLit's planes are always in top form, and the big jets, they're said to be safer than cars, yeah?"

She drew in a deep breath.

Damien opened the door, holding it for her.

Before passing through, though, Ravyn folded her arms and pressed one more time. "Just one last question," she said. "Why? It seems like an awful lot of money and effort just for a few stories."

Leaning a shoulder against the door, Damien was quiet. Then he said, "If I told you, you wouldn't believe me."

Lifting her chin, Ravyn said, "Try me."

Studying her, Damien narrowed his eyes before looking away, fingering the beads that hung loosely from the braided leather round his wrist. "Wild magic," he said finally. "It's returning to the world."

"Uh-huh." There was no committal in those words. Only an affirmation that she was listening to what he had to say.

"But there are people out there who want to stop it."

"Wild magic. People who want to stop it." Her voice was tinged with more than a bit of cynicism when she asked, "And how do we fit into this picture?"

His gray eyes looked into hers. "To make sure they don't."

Ravyn's smirk widened into a grin. "Right."

Damien shrugged even as the dark pooling of his eyes contradicted his nonchalance. "Becoming a part of all this? Probably one of the most important things you'll do in life."

It was hard to see that angle at the moment. More like the silliest thing she'd ever do in life. But it wasn't as if she was paying for any of it. Not financially, at least. In terms of emotional turmoil, though. That was a different story.

Then again, as Damien said – and here she glanced up at him – there were compensations.

But Ravyn kept these observations (especially the last) to herself choosing, with

some hesitation, to step across the threshold instead. Damien followed beside her, letting the
door close behind them with a click.

Part Two

Rock of the Fairies

Chapter Seven

As a girl, barefoot with flower-sprigged curls (curls which were just as apt to sport random bits of leaves, moss and fern fronds too), Ravyn loved to wander the woodland paths just beyond the village boundaries through what she was certain was the forest primeval filled with wild, star-dazzled pools and friendly, meandering brooks like the one she took to sitting by, conversing with the starflowers. Lessons on life, geology, the very nature of the universe and its shifting winds of history came from here. No one believed it, of course, when she told them what the flowers taught her. Except, perhaps, her mother and father.

Still back then Ravyn loved to share those observations from the town's forest with anyone, however skeptical, who cared to listen.

But that was long ago.

In the face of an ever-lurking world of economic "opportunity," career paths, and the societal imperative to become a useful member of the industrial-consumer economy, those wild ways of enchantment were curbed by well-meaning educators, paragons of mainstreaming, and she'd been whittled down to a sweet young thing with a dreamy bent for writing poetry and quaint stories full of quiet charm. But, most importantly from the educators' perspective, Ravyn had been redeemed enough from that fantasy world of hers to be at least moderately employable in any number of useful industries.

Given all this, driving back from the interview in the Hidden Mountains Ravyn full well understood what it would mean were she to return home from her visit there with tales for her neighbors of how well she was being paid to search out fairies and, as she assumed the position implied, remain vigilant for random acts of wild magic.

So Ravyn kept mum, sharing such a thing with only those closest to her.

Pyxi heard, of course.

Her parents, too – each of whom took it in stride as if such a thing were bound to happen with their daughter someday, leaving Ravyn more than a little nonplussed. Surely a job centered around tracking down magical beings was something about which to remark. Then again, everyone knew her parents were a law unto themselves. It should in no way surprise their only child that such things as the fairy-like and fantastical were taken as a matter akin to the basic nature of the universe.

Kaye redeemed them both, however, eyes popping wide enough to make up for the complacency of the parents' reaction, and Ravyn smiled to think she finally had a chance to verbally analyze the weirdness of this new position.

Until...

"Tell me more," Kaye urged, settling on Ravyn's futon with a bowl of popcorn in her lap, stockinged feet curled under her. "Damien can't really have been that handsome." At Ravyn's startled blink, she explained, "Your moony face gave it away. Are you sure it isn't just the French accent? You know, coloring things? Especially in retrospect?"

Ravyn was quite certain. But she only shrugged and didn't say so, fiddling with the eyelet lace on her sofa pillow.

Pyxi purred in her lap as if all was placed in the world exactly as it should be.

"Something's going on up there," Ravyn said instead, hoping to revive her original intent for the evening's chitchat.

"Really?" Kaye lifted a brow and nibbled another handful of popcorn. "Why do you say that?"

"Just something about the place. Secret doors. A hidden art gallery. Even a deluxe bunker."

"Deluxe bunker?" Kaye scrounged in her popcorn bowl for another handful.

"Bianca also said something about HQ being a safe place after certain assignments." Her eyes remained riveted on Kaye.

Kaye stopped nibbling the popcorn. "What does *that* mean?"

Quiet for a moment, Ravyn finally said what she'd been trying to ignore given the one or two newfound perks of her new position. "That I should be finding another job." So she'd returned to that possibility, had she?

"France is only a trial run," Kaye reminded her, but her interest wandered back to things she evidently deemed of greater import. "Did he really say he was enchanted to meet you?" she asked, another handful of popcorn disappearing.

Lips pressing together – though she wanted to firmly reiterate "They asked me to go looking for fairies!" – Ravyn willed herself into seeing things from her friend's perspective before she quietly replied, "Well, I don't exactly know French…"

It didn't seem to matter. "Enchanted" had to have been what he'd said. Or so explained Kaye. It was, after all, the closest thing to the knights of old – full of charm, courage, and abiding love – or so it was with such things as the girls they once were had dreamed.

Merely nodding as she picked at pillow lint and scratched Pyxi a little too enthusiastically for the feline's immediate comfort, Ravyn listened to Kaye's enthusiastic monologue. It required no effort to stay abreast of the wholly familiar topic. Ancient maids of around-thirty-something that they both were, neither had ever really grown beyond the romantic ideals of their girlish fancies. But both were learning as women in a modern world, finding a man to match was another thing altogether.

Though neither one had yet to meet him, each had spent time with her fair share of impostors.

In the end once Kaye went home, the house quiet again, Pyxi proved the most avid listener of all. Her human sighed over the lunacy of getting paid – or more to the point: having to hop on board a plane and fly far away – to investigate the existence of beings everyone knew did not exist. Pyxi reached with a silken paw to tap the palm of Ravyn's open hand as if in sympathy with her nervous plight.

Breath slowing to match Pyxi's purr, Ravyn closed her eyes. "Maybe just embrace the idea of infinite possibility?" Her fingers twined through cat fur as she mulled over the sudden inspiration, unquestioning in her assumption that this was a one-sided conversation. She could keep her mind open about such things as magic in the world, sure. At least just wide enough so logic and reason hadn't sufficient room to fall out.

The flying in a plane thing, though. That was an entirely different story. One whose resolution she wouldn't fully know until directly confronted with the metallic beast.

In all likelihood, unemployment still loomed in her immediate future.

A couple weeks later when MegaLit's elegant, black and gleaming SUV arrived – its motor so soft it had to be electric – ready to take Ravyn on the first leg of her journey to France, Kaye was on Ravyn's front porch. She didn't hide the fact that she'd undertaken the responsibility to assess and appraise her friend's new co-worker as he stepped out of the Escalade IQ. Damien's first act met with approval as he hoisted Ravyn's luggage into the back without hesitation or even a nudge in that direction.

Ostensibly Kaye had dropped by merely to make sure Pyxi wasn't traumatized by her mistress's departure, rare as those departures were. It didn't matter that Ravyn's parents – who lived in the spacious lot behind her own home and spoiled and petted the little cat just as much as Ravyn did – would be cat-sitting while she was gone. Moral support at the time of departure was, Kaye was certain, exactly what the much indulged feline needed.

So while Ravyn's dad gathered cat things from inside Ravyn's home, and Ravyn's mom made sure her daughter had enough snacks for the trip (returning from her own house a third time laden with more bags of Christmas cookies for Damien as well as the driver she'd spotted inside the MegaLit vehicle), Kaye stood with Pyxi on the porch watching the proceedings.

The tortoiseshell in question, seeming not at all distressed at Ravyn's preparations, purred graciously in Kaye's arms, eyes popping open only once to regard Ravyn with a serious cat stare when said human came to stand in farewell before her.

Ravyn gave Pyxi her favorite scratch behind the left ear. "Miss you, kit," she said.

Extending her neck forward, Pyxi sniffed Ravyn's nose as was her habit, licked its tip, then once again exhaled a happy sigh into the crook of Kaye's elbow.

One last ruffling of the velvet fur and Ravyn made her way down the steps, clambering into the vehicle while Damien held the door. She smiled slightly at him before settling onto the plushly upholstered seat.

"Keep an eye on those fairies!" Kaye loudly teased.

Ravyn flushed, eyeing Mrs. Dillon, a neighbor she'd known since childhood. The dainty and silver-haired lady had been sweeping the scanty remains of snow from her porch steps well onto twenty minutes now, neck craning to look anywhere but at the planks beneath her feet where, tiny but fierce, a Yorkie bounced about in a game of tag with the aimlessly meandering broom.

Damien gently shut Ravyn's door.

Ravyn rolled down the window, ready to wave goodbye, just in time to hear her father call, "Stay this side of any stone circles, dear! They can be tricky things."

In terms of her neighborhood reputation, not helping. Forever the fey young thing next door, on the spectrum of delightfully eccentric to outright insane the neighborhood assessment had no doubt plunged that morning in terms of Ravyn's mental well-being. Though there were more than a few who likely found the wealth displayed with the Escalade as proof she was on to something fruitful and so would forgive her any display of unsound mental peregrinations. She didn't like it, but there it was - eccentricity was tolerated in the rich but suspect in the financially insecure.

Inside the Cadillac the colors were professional and sober. But it was the immense display screen running along the dash, stretching from one side of the vehicle to the other, that seemed to dominate the interior, at least in the front. Readings from it were projected onto the windshield as if it were more of a computer monitor than a shield against onrushing things. Unlike her trusty but rusty steed, Ravyn doubted this vehicle's gas gauge – or charge-o-meter or whatever – had its fitful days. Still, she far preferred her little runabout to this specimen of opulence.

Instrumental music, relaxing and unobtrusive, played over the well-equipped speakers. Though not muzak, it carried a similar vibe. As the vehicle rolled away from the curb, the reality of what lay ahead settled in, oozing like melted lead to the bottom of her stomach. Even Damien, handing her important things as he spoke, wasn't alleviating the sensation.

"Your passport." A faint and pleasant scent of fresh cedar about him, Damien gave her a small navy blue booklet. "Expedited."

With a quick peek inside, it was clear her mugshot was only there to embarrass her. The coldly efficient blankness of the regimented lines inside the book fomented a wave of homesickness. Ravyn quietly placed the document in her lap.

Damien handed her a leather sleeve embossed with the MegaLit logo. "For your passport and anything else with a RFID chip." At her confused look, he explained, "They aren't supposed to be trackable from a distance, but this will keep you safe just in case."

That didn't enlighten matters any. And safe from what?

"And here. For you to look over." He handed her a leather file pouch, same embossed MegaLit logo on the front. "Should help the plane trip go more quickly."

The plane trip. Right. The less *that* was spoken of the more she was likely to actually get on it when the time came. Ravyn rifled through what looked to be a hundred pages of text on La Roche aux Fées then closed the folder. She'd already done her research, but Damien was right. She'd need it for the plane trip.

More papers in hand, Damien looked apologetic. "Just a few more. Our itinerary. More or less. Except for the flights, it's flexible enough." With a crooked smile, he glanced up, dark eyes under dark hair. "We have time to relax, enjoy things."

Her eyebrows knit together.

"Worried?"

"About what?"

Damien shrugged. "The plane. First times aren't easy." He smiled again. "But I haven't crashed yet."

Ravyn shoved a hand in her coat pocket, gripping the lucky stone there. A unicorn stone her mom called it when giving it to her years ago. It came with her promise that it held magical powers to heal and protect. Didn't seem like it could hurt to bring it along on her first flight ever.

"Don't worry," he added. "The first bit is on our Bombardier. With Mega-Lit's maintenance, it's probably the safest one you'll ever get on."

"Is it a big plane?" Her voice was faint as she imagined being swallowed by a cavernous machine.

Damien shrugged. "It's a private jet. But it handles the winds and turbulence like the big planes."

Ravyn's brows pulled together so tightly her forehead hurt. Not that she'd ever given it a moment's thought, but if she had it would seem to her small planes were the preferred way to fly. Less people. More direct access to the pilot. Maybe not so high in the sky, although falling from one thousand feet as opposed to seven thousand or whatever probably didn't make that much of a difference now that she considered the physics of the thing. If small planes were more dangerous, she didn't want to know about it.

There were so many ruts on the road leading to the local airport, even the sturdily built, well-equipped, luxury vehicle jerked about. The airport itself was rather less port and more field with two small hangars and a landing strip surrounded by spruce woods. Ravyn clutched the armrest as she spotted the MegaLit logo on a smallish (more like juvenile giant) plane. It sat ready on its wheels, waiting like the shiny metallic beast she'd imagined, complacently cognizant that swallowing her whole was only one small part of its vastly important destiny.

But only if she let it.

Outside the SUV dark woods bordering the field pressed close. Behind them, the road out disappeared into snow laden trees.

"Last chance," Damien said softly, eyes not meeting hers.

Ravyn's ragged breath fogged the vehicle window. She let go the armrest, fingering the seatbelt buckle.

Chapter Eight

Staring through the window of the Escalade at the smallish MegaLit jet as it squatted on the airfield, Ravyn was dimly aware, like one is aware of the subtle hiss of background static, that people – vague, dark shapes outside – scurried about unloading the SUV. As she emerged from the vehicle, time seemed to expand, space to thicken.

By sheer force of will she moved her legs toward the waiting plane, hesitating at the base of the boarding steps. With a quick breath in, she hurried up them. Then stopped abruptly.

A woman had moved to stand in the plane's doorway. Bright pink hair pulled back in a loosely plaited French braid, wearing glasses, a black turtleneck, and jeans, at first she simply frowned at Ravyn, blue eyes not quite unfriendly. But not exactly friendly either. After an awkward silence during which Ravyn shifted her feet on the steps precisely three times, the woman resumed chewing gum. "Stacy," she said. "Welcome aboard." She moved back into the plane, taking a seat around which were strewn several laptops, computer cords and other tech paraphernalia Ravyn couldn't begin to guess at.

"Um, Ravyn, " Ravyn offered, her smile a gingerly diplomatic attempt. But, not receiving a similar response in return (Stacy having begun to rapidly pound on a keyboard as if the characters on the keys were sooner or later bound to make their escape) Ravyn instead sought a seat near a window and made herself at home. Settling her winter coat over the back of the chair, she was careful to remove the unicorn stone and place it in a pocket of the cardigan she wore. It was only when she sat down that Ravyn remembered all her luggage back in the SUV.

Cheeks warm, Ravyn minced back down the short and narrow aisle only to run head on into Damien as he opened the door, her bags in hand.

"I completely – so totally – I'm sorry." Flustered, she dove to grab one of her bags than thought it might be easier for both concerned if she just let Damien continue on his trajectory into the plane and hopped back only to crunch down on somebody's foot standing behind her. She turned around having to look up and up again at the blonde-haired man whose foot she'd just smushed.

"You must be Ravyn." He was handsome with the kind of smile that indicated full awareness of the fact while simultaneously dismissing this state of nature as irrelevant – for the moment. He shook her hand. "It's Trevor," he said gripping her elbow as well. "But friends call me Trev." Then he reached beside her for one of the bags and backpacks Damien had tossed into the cabin.

Damien, still just outside the door, made his way back to the bottom of the steps, grabbing several duffles to deposit inside the doorway of the airplane before heading down again for the last of the luggage in the Escalade.

Not sure whether her presence was helpful or hindersome, Ravyn picked up her own duffle bags and backpack, hauling them to her chosen seat. Masterful air-traveler that she was, she tossed the luggage on the floor beside her seat, wondering why they designed planes with so little room for passengers' stuff. Figuring she'd just have to deal with the mess of her jumbled bags, Ravyn determinedly but awkwardly clambered over them to get to a window seat.

Stacy looked over at her, glanced above Ravyn's head, then looked at her again. "Uh, you know you can just put them in the overhead compartments, right?"

"Right," Ravyn said, hair falling out of its barrette, coat twisted slightly askew. She patted

114

her bags as she sat on them mid-clamber. "The more they're squashed, the better they'll fit, eh?" But her weak defense failed to stimulate confidence even in herself.

Stacy went back to typing.

Trevor looked Ravyn's way and winked.

Ravyn tried to smile as she wrestled with the overhead compartment, the last bag finally squishing in beside the others.

All luggage accounted for, Damien stepped inside, neatly placing his own in a nearby compartment – no squashing needed – before taking the seat beside hers.

Again Ravyn noted the faint and pleasing scent as of fresh-cut cedar as he did so, and she sat down quickly, rooting in her purse for something she was sure she needed even if she couldn't quite put a name on it yet.

"They're part of the team," he said, answering the question she hadn't yet thought to think. "Trevor, he does security mostly. And Stacy..." He looked over his shoulder, lowering his voice. "She's not completely sold on the whole wild magic thing, thinks we're all..." He gave a low whistle. "A bit off."

Noting Stacy as a possible if improbable kindred spirit, Ravyn asked, "What's she do then?"

"Tech support."

"And with Trevor – we actually need security?" Stacy's tech part she got. Of course. But a security guard? Then her upper lip curled into a smug smirk. "Don't tell me. He keeps the poltergeists at bay."

"If only." Looking at her sideways, Damien added, "Some people, they're not so friendly, yeah? If you think of *Indiana Jones*, somebody's always out for the same thing. Take out a lot of the drama and the action and it can be the same for us sometimes."

Ravyn's grin vanished.

"But not this trip." He gave her a tight smile. "Not on your first time out. Nobody can capture the fairies, eh? So nobody will be trying."

"I wasn't worried." As if she wasn't that very moment working to smooth her pursed lips and peel her cramping fingers from the armrest. Besides – and the reminder did her good – she was only a writer. It wasn't as if she'd have anything of value to offer a nefarious treasure seeker.

Except, she supposed...

At least eventually, perhaps...

Information.

Didn't OSHA protect workers against such things somehow?

A chill crept up her spine.

The pilot's preparatory call before take-off filtered to her as if through a thick fog before Ravyn's attention snapped back to the moment looming before her. She quickly fastened her seatbelt, trying not to appear hurried as if she were rushing to be snugly buckled in before a single wheel crept even a millimeter off the ground or something.

Movement stirred in her gut. Snow-covered ground outside the window started moving as the muffled, grinding sound of engines reverberated through the cabin, their pitch increasing with the plane's speed. Ravyn closed her eyes, clutching at the armrests again and wishing she'd looked up Lamaze breathing techniques – or anything else like it – to distract her thoughts.

A hand closed over hers.

She looked up.

It was Damien. "Give it a moment. Things won't be so bad."

His smile was sweet as he pressed her hand briefly before letting go.

There was a buzzing in her ears. She shut her eyes again. It only seemed to accentuate the flip of her belly as the plane tilted, finding lift.

Curiosity, though, had to know things. Gripping the unicorn stone in her coat pocket, one by one Ravyn released the fingers of her other hand from the armrest, flexing her hand when all digits were free. Then she opened her eyes peering out the window at the world below.

They were high. The plane had leveled. But the altitude was neither awe-inspiring nor, once she got over the initial shock, even fright-inducing. It just did. There was the snow-covered ground, small patches of brown peeking through. Houses smaller than cake décor on a vanilla frosted cupcake sparsely dotted the landscape. And everything slipped by so slowly.

"Like I said, not so bad." Damien watched her carefully.

"No. No, I guess not. Not terribly." Ravyn's words were breathy. The buzzing had diminished but her head felt like a helium balloon on a loosely tethered string as she looked out windows across the aisle. One of the Great Lakes glittered below them.

"Huron?" She nodded in its direction.

"Michigan," Damien said. "We just flew over the Straits."

"Milwaukee airport? Maybe Chicago?" Her brain seemed incapable of forming complex sentences at the moment.

Damien nodded. "Think you can handle Chicago's O'Hare?"

She took the softness in his eyes as confidence she could.

But Ravyn wasn't so sure. Thumb running over its smooth depression in the middle, she took the unicorn stone out of her pocket. It didn't look like much. Roughly textured outside of the worn depression. Pale grayish pink with the faintest streaks of lapis lazuli blue.

"It's more than just a 'dumb stone,' " her mom had said to Ravyn's child self many years ago. "Rocks always are. And this stone in particular. All the love and protection of unicorns can be found in one such as this. It may look like many another rock, but see?" She'd turned out the lights. A galaxy of glowing embers blossomed inside the stone. "It'll help with your nightmares." Turning the lights back on, her mom put a finger to her lips. "But this is just a family thing," she said. Her words were stern. "Tell no one."

Whatever its backstory, the stone worked. The bad dreams lessened in frequency. Though even now Ravyn could still wake in the middle of the night, adrenalin pumping like a starburst in flight, fear and futility almost palpable flavors in her mouth.

The little rock had gotten a lot of use over the years.

Putting it away again, she caught Damien's gaze.

He didn't say anything, only crooked a slight sort of smile at her before returning to watch the lake slide endlessly by beyond the windows.

Truth be told, the flight was rather, well, tame. The engines continued to drone on without the occasional stop and go that broke the monotony of driving a car long distance. Here and there a seagull glided with them before disappearing, and the slowly changing cloudscape offered some visual diversion. Early in the flight an occasional island briefly emerged on the waters, mildly interesting in its aerially-observed features.

But nothing observed from her aery bower was as riveting as driving a car down a winding road through an old pine forest, deer bounding into the wood, pileateds bobbing a crossing overhead while a porcupine might waddle into the hidey-hole of a thatch of roadside grass.

The fact that Ravyn had forgotten about reviewing the information on La Roche aux Fées, though, was an indication she was more riveted with the flight than she thought.

The undulating lake below making her thirsty, Ravyn sipped from her water bottle as Trevor took a seat in front of them, his thick blonde hair all that was visible above the headrest. Moments later Trevor spun the seat around to face them.

Ravyn spilled water down her blouse.

Damien settled a sneakered foot on top of one knee, thumb tapping absently on his leg.

"Stace," Trevor called to their other co-worker as Ravyn did her best to gracefully blot up her small spill with a tissue. Settling back in the cushiony seat, Trevor stretched out his black denim clad legs before him. "Come on up here and get to know our new colleague." He smiled broadly at Ravyn as he spun the empty chair next to him to face her and Damien. "Stace can be a hedgehog, but don't let it bug you."

"Damien says you do security." Ravyn leaned forward, carefully pulling her cardigan close to cover the water stain. "Anything I should be worried about?"

Trevor glanced at Damien. "Nothing Damien hasn't already told you."

Damien held Trevor's look for a moment before he turned to Ravyn, shrugging. "International travel has its risks." Damien's voice was steady. "But like I said, this trip nothing's on the radar. After Chicago we won't even be using the Bombardier."

"Yeah, Stace and I need it," Trevor said as if offering an insightful aside.

"*Our* trip," Damien continued, "it should be a low key in-and-out. See if what Bianca, she, uh, has heard about has any truth to it – "

Ravyn smiled with good humor, imagining, just for one ridiculous moment, what the world would think if they were to actually discover fairies.

"— and come home. A good test run for you." Damien fiddled with the denim fringe around a small hole in the knee of his jeans.

Quietly grumbling indecipherable things as she joined them, Stacy sat next to Trevor, perched on the edge of the seat he'd prepped for her, posture ramrod straight. "So what now?" she asked them all. "We talk favorite colors, foods and superheroes?" With a tone that suggested she'd find solitude in a deep, dark hole offered more convivial company, she asked, "Trekker or Star Wars?"

Caught off guard, Ravyn pushed into better posture herself. "Uh, neither?"

"Cake or pie?"

"Both?"

"Uh-huh. Favorite color?"

"Is that your idea of friendly conversation? I'd call that interrogation." Trevor's lip curled. "And they say women are the communicators."

"It's alright," Ravyn hastened to add. The last thing she wanted was the only other woman on the four-person team resenting her. "And it's opal green," she said, smiling. "My favorite color."

But Stacy didn't smile back. Instead she looked at Trevor, chewed her gum a couple times, and sighed. "Are we done?"

"Yeah," he said with a grumpy grin. "Go back to whatever cramped and stone-cold cave you were curled up in."

"Whatev." Stacy left without further comment.

Leaning close to Ravyn, Damien said softly, "She's, how do you say, an acquired taste. But she's not so bad once you get to know her."

"Just be patient," Trevor added. "Really patient in your case. I mean…" He looked apologetically at Damien.

Damien ran a finger along his chin, shaking his head slightly at Trevor.

Trevor shrugged, dropped his gaze for a momentary study of the plane aisle, and didn't expand on his point.

The look Damien gave Ravyn seemed genuinely concerned. "Ravyn's had a lot thrown at her."

"Alright." Trevor rose from his seat. "But I'm just a few seats back," he told her. "If you feel you want some *real* conversation."

With a nod to Trevor on his departure, Damien dug a book out of his bag. The title was something in French.

Returning to gaze out the window, Ravyn shifted more than once in her seat, finding it difficult to settle with the seatbelt strapping her in before she finally inclined the seat, grabbed her winter coat and plumped it into a reasonably comfortable pillow, cheek resting against its soft wool. But her eyes remained wide watching the the lake crawl by, glittering waters turquoise in the sun.

If it was France, fairies and Neolithic dolmens this time, what would the next assignment entail? If she chose to accept the position, that is. Practically in her own backyard and all as it was, the stone circle in the Straits of Mackinac had grabbed her attention from the moment Bianca introduced it back in the Hidden Mountains. A circle there, under such deep water, had to be many millennia older than even the dolmens in France.

She leaned forward, pressing her forehead to the window, its glass cold. But she didn't draw back. Maybe if she looked hard enough, shafts of sunlight might plumb the bottom of the water's depths, revealing things long buried in time. Things she'd not yet thought to search for.

Chapter Nine

O'Hare Airport – its digital signs flashing flight names, departures, arrivals and cancellations thick as flurries in a snowstorm, its din of PA announcements and a hundred conversations, its antiseptic smells and scents of leather, cologne, hair shampoo and just plain old human sweat – rushed at Ravyn as she stepped from the runway and into the terminal.

Several thousand people milled, hurried, stood, sat all in this one complex. Two point three seven million this month last year. Seventy-six thousand this day last year. Three thousand an hour.

She'd looked it up.

Caught in their wake, Ravyn blinked, realizing Damien was saying something to her.

Gently taking her by the elbow, he led her over to a quieter corner of a seating area. Like an eddy at the the edge of a tumultuous river, here the conversation was a low hubbub, the PA only slightly less booming.

Ravyn could breathe again. "That was worse than the plane," she said so quietly Damien had to ask her to repeat it.

"Coming out of the bush into crowds isn't easy," he said.

Ravyn looked at him. "Where are you from anyway?" A "townie," no one had ever thought of her as living in the bush.

Damien surprised her, but not in the vein she expected. "Québec City," he answered. "In a way."

She stared. And completely forgot her point.

"That's in Québec," he added, as if seeing the need for an explanation.

"I know it's in Quebec," she said, recovering, though not enough to pronounce the name of his homeland properly. "Québec, I mean. And I just meant I thought you were – "

"From France?"

Her grin was sheepish.

Trevor, empty-handed, found them then. Stacy came behind. Bags and cases hung about her like a walking techie holiday tree, wired earbuds stuck in both ears.

Damien raised an eyebrow at Trevor. "Wouldn't hurt to offer her help, yeah?"

"Been there, done that. I value my body parts too much to ask again."

Conversation lapsed into time schedules. With three hours to spare, Ravyn looked around the terminal. She'd prefer to be taking off on the MegaLit jet like their two coworkers soon would be rather than stay so long in the press of such a crowd.

The sound of voices turned tinny again, her vision tunneling, head as light as a feather. The rest was simply a blur of faces, queue lines, scanners and talking uniforms. Damien walked her through it all, keeping a gentle hand at her elbow or on the small of her back. Not something she'd typically welcome. Given the circumstances, though, it was like a grounding wire in a lightning storm.

They were walking out of Burger King, Ravyn grateful for the familiarity of a burger and fries, when their jet pulled up outside the all-window walls, presumably aligning for boarding. "AirFrance" it said in big, bold blue letters along its side

She had an urge to flee.

Or freeze.

Either was far preferable to boarding that monstrosity. The idea of its taking to the skies was plainly a direct contradiction of anyone's common sense understanding of physics. Or should be at any rate.

The unicorn stone in Ravyn's pocket found itself in fair danger of pulverization. A bead of perspiration trickled down her back.

Frankly, later there remained little more than a blurred patch in Ravyn's memory of what came next. Boarding. Take-off. The actual flight itself yielded only a vague recollection of pearly leather seats, sunset glow along the planet's rim, and a star-studded deepness to the darkening sky. All enveloped within the dampened noise of powerful engines holding them aloft.

It was their silence that woke her.

Seats, some bathed in the warm glow of nighttime LEDs, sat empty around her. She could feel the pulse in her neck start to throb. Trying to think, to understand, her mind only offered phrases like "Bermuda Triangle" and "Twilight Zone."

It was then she noticed Damien's backpack. Placed neatly on his seat, the skateboarding magazine rolled and stuffed into a side pocket. His jacket lay on top.

Slowly the soft murmur of subdued conversation, shuffling feet, and thudding compartment doors filtered into her soundscape.

Certain now that Damien hadn't just taken off (or been sucked into a mysterious vortex) leaving her to fend for herself, Ravyn straightened her clothes. As she was pulling her hair back into a quick ponytail, Damien came up to stand behind her, elbow on the top of the seat's headrest as he popped a handful of peanuts in his mouth.

"Morning," he said, then offered the bag of nuts to her. "Hungry?" At her polite refusal, he folded the bag, stuffed it in his backpack and grabbed his coat as he smiled. "Welcome to France."

It wasn't until they boarded the train, the bustle of French conversations infusing the surroundings, and left the city that things began to feel actually French.

Outside the train windows, small farm fields blurred by, dominating the landscape. But the train sped past it all so fast, her stomach rebelled, and she had to focus on things less whizzy near at hand.

Pulling out the file pouch on La Roche aux Fées from her backpack, she flipped through the packet. Having done her research prior to the trip, much of it wasn't new info. "You've been to this place before, I'm sure," she said to Damien.

"Brittany. Not La Roche."

Her eyebrows rose. "Really? I guess I just sort of thought La Roche itself was a spot you'd have studied a lot or something."

"Not this one, no." He looked out the window at the passing farm fields. "There's more than a thousand dolmens here though. So, yeah, I've been to the region a few times. The place has a lot of energy."

"Energy? Like ley lines?" Her forehead creased as she frowned, unconvinced. "I guess that could explain things with the dolmens, what with the burials and all. But I don't know."

His tone was skeptical too. "Ley lines? Can't say I've ever run into any." His smile was apologetic. "Not yet anyway, so who knows. The dolmen, though, you really think its only purpose, it was for burials?"

Ravyn shrugged. "Well, yeah."

A corner of his mouth lifted a little, and he leaned slightly toward her. "Why haul forty-ton rocks just to make a tomb? Brittany five thousand years ago is too far back for a civilization with all its, how do you say, hierarchies and authoritarianism."

"Wouldn't you do such a thing if you believed it gave your loved ones a boost in the next life?"

"Point taken," he said.

"And they *were* civilized," Ravyn countered, feeling compelled to defend the Neolithic. Her chin jutted forward.

"That word, civilized...I wouldn't use it as a compliment."

Civilization did have a bit of a citified air about it. Civilization. *Civitas.* City. "Fair enough," she agreed.

Outside, fields and hedgerows kept pace with the train, shifting into blocks of housing. A ballfield or two made an appearance. Putting the folder on La Roche aside again, Ravyn prodded at the unfinished bit of their conversation. "How do *you* think they built these things? And why?"

Damien replied with a shrug and not a little characteristic evasion. "Who knows? But at La Roche, they say the fairies do."

"Fairies. Right." Skeptical that any sensible explanation of things was within reach at the moment, Ravyn returned to leafing through the info packet, darting an occasional glance out the window where a winding river had meandered in, apartment buildings sprouting along its banks. Powerlines swooped down, running parallel to the tracks. Eventually she had to prod, "If you don't think the dolmens' only use was as tombs, what do you think La Roche was used for?"

"Human sacrifice."

Ravyn's head jerked as she turned to stare at him.

"Joking." Damien grinned. "You know how some people are. Because the dolmen's connected to a tribal culture, they think it must have been for something ungodly." His upper lip lifted slightly. "*Ça, c'est typique.*" It seemed more muttered to himself, but he caught her quizzical look. "Typical of them," he explained.

She settled back into her seat, resolving to download a language app and learn some French. Or at least just have the translator handy – it should have been something she considered before departing on this trip but other things had loomed larger. Like the plane. Fairies. And other such inconsequential stuff.

The train pulled along old high-rise buildings. Shipping containers flashed by just before tall metal fences sporting colorful graffiti blocked the view. It took until then before she thought to ask, leaning forward again, "Typical of who?"

Collecting his coat and things, Damien didn't answer.

Hesitant to press, Ravyn lost the chance as the train pulled into Rennes station.

Their small little rental Fiat was made for the curves of the road that lay ahead. So narrow it seemed impossible two vehicles could pass abreast, the backcountry byway wove a spell as it wound its way through the bucolic French countryside. Picket fences, draped with the dried memory of summer's flowering vines, lined the roadside lending an extra dash of old world charm.

So too did tidy stonework walls, a few crumbling in disrepair. Country homes, neat and compact and built of clay or stone, bunched in tiny neighborhoods where woodsy groves flourished – but only in small clusters as if not daring to invade the parade of snow-speckled farm fields all around. Every few miles another pocket-sized community, some as old as a millennium, interrupted the fields and their hedgerows.

"You know," Ravyn began with a suddenness that made Damien jerk the wheel. She clutched the dash even as she asked, "Would France allow some pipeline to just go through one of these old places?"

Having cleared his throat as he recovered from his driving error, however forgivable it may have been, Damien considered. "Probably not, no."

She nodded. "So why do we allow it? I looked up that Ice Age circle in the Straits of Mackinac." Ravyn let go of the dash.

Her partner was quiet.

Pursing her lips, Ravyn continued, "You know it's going to be obliterated by that tunnel they want to build."

"For the oil pipeline, that's the one you mean?"

"All the oldness around here." As a stone fence rolled by, reddish lichen clambering along its length, Ravyn stopped talking a moment to simply watch it pass instead. "It makes you think. How did so many dolmens make it through thousands of years if people didn't care?"

"They didn't all make it through," he said. "But you're right in general. Maybe because France, it doesn't have a history of conquest to rationalize very much. At least not in the same way we might be used to back home, yeah?"

Eyes sidling sideways, taking his measure, Ravyn shifted in her seat.

It wasn't difficult to know when they drew near their destination. One clear clue was the townhall just outside of Essé, its entryway draped with evergreen bows. A sign above these proclaimed Pays La Roche aux Fées. Or Rock of the Fairies Country – translation courtesy of the new app she'd downloaded while waiting for the rental car back at the Rennes train station.

Rue des Fées or Fairy's Road, was another hint they'd arrived. A simple street budding out from the heart of downtown, it ran along a line of old redstone buildings and curved out of sight as the road reached a copse of small woods at the edge of town.

Plus as they slowed for a stop at the intersection the GPS started beeping. With a glance at the screen, Damien nodded at Fairy's Road. "Our inn, it's down there. So's La Roche."

Until the computer stepped in like that it was almost as if they'd discovered a celebrated land of fairies all on their own.

They both agreed to head first to La Roche for an initial foray in the daylight. After a proper lunch stop, at Au Marché des La Roche aux Fées. Though Damien said it was only a neighborhood "*dep*" – by which, he'd gone on to explain, he meant convenience store – it advertised burgers and fries all day.

If that alone wasn't enough, it sported a shop sign with a slender blue fairy wrapped in a magical starry swirl sitting on top a simple dolmen. Blue holiday lights, lit despite the daytime, circled the sign.

Ravyn was intrigued and, feeling bold, she double-checked that her translator app was prepped and ready. No better time to take on the task of ordering in French as best she could – even as Damien stood nearby, intently studying the floor as she did so. Eventually, however, she gave in, capitulating back to her native language to ask for ketchup with the fries. "Actual French fries," she said quietly to Damien, biting her lip to prevent a giggle.

"*Voudriez-vous de la mayo avec vos frites, madame?*" asked the woman behind the counter, her look one of long endurance.

Having closed the app, Ravyn looked to Damien for a translation. And when she got it, she could think of no reason why someone would ask if she'd want mayo with her fries. "*Non, merci.* Ketchup, *s'il vous plaît.*" So impressed was she with saying essentially an entire two sentences in French – without her app, no less – she nearly missed the oddly disapproving look on the woman's face.

Nevertheless, a sandwich and fries-with-ketchup later, she and Damien toodled down Fairy's Road, bypassing their inn for the night to head onward a couple miles further to the official drive for La Roche aux Fées.

"Where are all the trees?" she asked even as they drove through a small gathering of ancient oak. "I mean, the vast expanse of wild ones?" What with words like "fairies" and "wild magic" being bandied about, the impression lent had certainly been one of visiting a site in the hinterlands of the French wilderness. Wild magic seemed as if it was synonymous with none other than...wildness. Magnificent trees all around. Human civilization miles and miles away. The ancient world preserved and writ large, all its magic allure visible with every passing glance, present in every winding wisp of air.

Even as he drove to the monument's parking lot, Damien looked about at the trees rising toward the blue sky, but he didn't reply to her question right away.

As they pulled in, a small, dark brown visitors' center was visible, squatting at the head of the parking area. Elegant evergreen garland and cute red shutters offset its rather mundane appearance.

"They've probably been gone quite a while," he said eventually, the car idling.

"Who?" The visitor center did look closed. And they were the only car in the parking lot. But Ravyn was learning not to assume the obvious with Damien. "You don't mean the fairies."

"It's a thought. Forest fairies, they do like the forests."

Ravyn softly snorted without meaning to, covering it with a delicate cough.

"But I meant the trees. Rome probably started the clearing for fuel. Then, not coincidentally, to get rid of the tribes. The woods would have given them independence." As he turned off the engine, a quiet settled about them.

Damien's points were actually pretty similar to some research she'd done for a romantasy a couple years earlier, one Bev felt it best not to publish. "Too much historical critique," Bev had said. A critique was there, true – how could it not be, given the subject matter? - but Ravyn had thought she'd made it oblique. Evidently not enough to make it publishable, at least by her old publisher's standards. "Even so, the trees should have grown back by now," Ravyn pointed out. "And be ancient woods. Especially around sites like these."

"Even after Rome there came the feudal lords, if you remember. And certain Christian authorities whose loyalty, it was more to feudal values than to any teachings of Jesus."

"You mean, declaring it God's work to clear the forests?" Ravyn frowned. "How did it make sense to people? Even in their own cosmology, hurting any part of Creation hurts a part of its Creator."

"I don't suppose rationality really matters if your goal, it's to build petty empires."

"By gaining control of a people, you mean."

"And from there the rest is, how do you say today, the way they spin it. Messaging. PR."

Tilting her chin, Ravyn studied him. "Not many people know this stuff."

Eyes hooded, Damien ran a thumb over the braided leather round his wrist. "There's always a reason if history's suppressed.

And didn't she know it. It was a history even Bev hadn't been willing to take on with Ravyn's unpublished story – at least not so directly. "With forests, people can escape feudal control."

"Without..." Damien pulled the keys. "Well, *you* know."

Each glanced sideways at the other, cheeks reddening as their eyes met. Academic indeed. So, Bev had been right. "Maybe we should go on the lecture circuit." Ravyn's voice was gentle in its teasing.

Smiling a little, Damien turned his attention to the land outside.

With a slow unfastening of her seatbelt Ravyn surveyed their surroundings as well. In sum there couldn't be much more than an acre of the old oaks surrounded by windswept vineyards dusted in snow. It was a pretty place, sure, but in a very cultivated, civilized way.

"I know fairies don't exist," she began. "But if they did, why would any who love the wilderness come back here?" She reached for her water bottle in the center console between them.

His thumb tapped the steering wheel. "It's probably not the source, this dolmen. Places like these are usually connected to wild energies somewhere else."

"Ley lines this time?"

"Nothing so geometric, no. This thing, it's a spirit-connection, yeah? Like a pond in the woods. The pond is connected to everything that happens along the stream feeding into it. If something really is happening here – "

"Fairies?" Ravyn chided, eyes rolling.

He quirked a smile. "If something magical's happening here, we need to find what or where this place is connected to. From there, we can find what caused the resurgence."

"Resurgence?"

"Of wild magic."

"I'm confused."

"Hold on to your little knit hat." His smile widened into a grin carrying a hint of mischief. "What we do can be fun, but it gets crazy. Eventually, though, things make sense. At least usually."

Drawing a breath, Ravyn put aside her confusion – not to mention skepticism – and just went with the crazy ideas Damien was suggesting. For the moment.

So. Wild magic. Somehow puddling here.

She couldn't see why.

But then she stepped out of the car. And the door hung open behind her, forgotten.

Chapter Ten

There were places Ravyn had visited in life that held something particularly sacred similar to the way a curled leaf cups fallen rain. It could be felt in the way the mist touched her skin or a wind played with her hair. Mossy rocks suggested fairy haunts, like two boulders in a vernal pool sheltered beneath a stalwart hemlock bough. As did spring violets spilling down between the roots of a towering basswood along a woodland creek.

Sometimes it was simply the quality of quiet that held sway there, a whispering of worlds unseen. Of love vast as a starlit sky.

La Roche didn't carry this same beauty. But it held echoes of it.

Damien, hands in his jean pockets, leaned against the little Fiat. Shoulders loose, the faint lines on his forehead nearly imperceptible even in the sunlight, he nodded toward a poster on the door of the visitor center. "Looks like they have a Solstice thing. Bonfire at dawn. Hot chocolate."

Together they walked the narrow sidewalk skirting the closed building, past a couple of paintings, or maybe they were charcoal sketches, that hung on the exterior wall. One was of a village scene, the land boasting only a scattering of sapling trees in the background. The other of a group of people, a man directing something at the center. Though a plaque pronounced these as depicting "Daily life in the Neolithic," neither matched Ravyn's idea of the time period, not the least because of the large numbers of people and small numbers of trees.

But what seemed a mundane, everyday tourist center was transformed as the concrete sidewalk ended at a dirt path, bisecting a well kept lawn just behind the building. Large oaks loomed on the other side of the lawn, ancient sentries crowding a structure made of stone cut to an impossible size.

As they drew near, it was clear the structure itself was nearly twice as tall as Damien, each stone more than three feet thick making the dolmen almost twenty feet wide. And somehow it charged the energy in the air. Not like a lightning storm ready to spark. More like the feel of an immense body of water, moving, present, ancient with depths so deep as to be unplumbed. The sheer enormity of the dolmen made Ravyn slow her pace, drawing several deep breaths as if the oxygen were being sucked from the outdoor space. Or maybe pressed out by the thick cut horizontal slabs that balanced heavily on top the vertical stone supports.

"You feel it too?" Damien's voice was low as he slowed his pace, matching hers.

As if pressed by some sort of mystical g-force, Ravyn found it difficult to nod in reply.

She stopped at the edge of a stone pillar framing the entryway to the interior and craned her neck to see inside. Despite the awkward position, it was far preferable to standing directly in front of the dolmen. There was something terribly imperious about the monument's immensity, grand as it was. Like an overwhelming force. Not malevolent. Just overwhelming. Ravyn wasn't sure she quite felt up to a direct confrontation with it at the moment and so avoided the threshold.

Inside the light was dusky. Dimly gold sunlight slanted through narrow gaps between the rock slabs. It highlighted trickles of green moss running along cracks in the stone, nestling in shadowed crannies.

Creeping forward, reaching the threshold Ravyn hesitated again. Tendrils of the chilled interior slowly coiled about her, wafting on a faint breeze.

Damien, however, walked in without hesitation – albeit cautiously. Several more people could have stood abreast of him with room to spare. The air smelled damp.

Although she had no doubt there was another explanation, it was understandable now why so many thought fairy magic essential to the dolmen's construction. "What are we missing?" She spoke hardly above a murmur.

"Sorry?" Damien was abstracted as he made his way back to her.

"Surely with all our engineering know-how, we can figure out how they built this way back then."

He ran a thumb across his chin, eyes squinting slightly as he looked down at her.

Ravyn noted he hadn't shaved in a while.

"Still thinking this, it's a human construct?" he asked.

Her answer, though definitive in her own mind, was verbally non-committal.

As Damien settled back on his heels and removed the lens cap from his camera to snap several shots from the front of the dolmen, Ravyn glanced at him again, trying to catch a glimmer of amusement in his demeanor. But there was none. After several minutes, frowning, he lowered the camera.

Hesitant to pry, Ravyn finally asked, "What is it?" in a voice low enough he could ignore her if he chose.

His too was soft in reply. "These stones, there's something about them." He took a photo of the entrance to the dolmen, the horizontal headstone large enough to weigh many tens of tons.

"You know how many?"

Damien shook his head.

"We should count them."

His glance swung to her. "Count them? You and me?"

"Sure."

Damien dropped his gaze, fiddling with the camera.

Having nothing better to do than stand and gawp (at the stones, of course, not the photographer), Ravyn started walking north in the afternoon's waning light of watery mauve and golds, counting stones as she went. "One, two…" She touched each one as she passed, the hard, granular surface a reassurance that the stone at least was real despite all the webs of fantasy woven around it.

From the corner of her eye, she saw Damien slowly rise to his feet and start to circle south on the other side. Moments later she heard, "*Catre, cinq…*"

"Forty-two," they both announced simultaneously when they met back at the entrance.

Damien blinked. "*Vraiment*? I mean, you're sure?"

She shrugged. "Sure, I'm sure."

His face flushed.

"At least we know something, right?" It didn't seem much. At this point with La Roche aux Fées, Ravyn was willing to take it. But she frowned as Damien shrugged and starting walking away.

"I guess," he said, voice fading as he reached the lawn on the way back to the parking lot. "But it's only a number."

"Uh-huh." Her assertion, though, wasn't very certain having little clarity on the reason for the strain that had suddenly popped up in the conversation, at least on Damien's end. She hurried to catch up with his long strides.

The light grew even more dim with the approach of a mackerel sky. They were the last of the visitors for the day, apparently, as no one else had arrived since they'd pulled in. Ravyn pulled her jacket collar close against the chill breeze. Damien stuffed his hands in his coat pockets, intently observing the vegetation and terrain as if looking for clues to something.

Back in the little car, he put the key in the ignition, but held off on turning it to look at Ravyn. "Where did they say the stone comes from?"

"Um," she reached into the backseat, pulling the pouch of information from her backpack along with her laptop containing her own saved research. "Here." She handed Damien the papers while she began searching her computer files.

It was a few minutes before Damien answered his own question, "The forest of Le Theil-de-Bretagne. About five, six kilometers from here. Could be something's happening there." He looked around. "I don't think the catalyst comes from here. Though I could be wrong."

The Theil forest sounded familiar. But something else nagged her. She skimmed quickly through her saved websites.

"This says the fairies brought the stones in their aprons from the Theil." Damien put the papers away. "Stories say they left a couple on the way, somewhere between here and the Theil Forest."

Suppressing her inner skeptic, Ravyn closed her laptop. "Alrighty then," she said with resignation. "What's next?"

"Before the fairy's Solstice fire tomorrow night?" He started the car. "Maybe check out the Theil forest in the morning. Maybe tonight see what the locals think. "

"Not the pubs." Her heart sank as she bit off a yawn. She didn't like bars.

"A café then?"

Cafés were only marginally better being as they could be just as crowded with people. But at least they were sober people.

Ravyn almost contained a second yawn, but not enough Damien failed to notice. "The Theil and whatever else, it can wait until after the Solstice tomorrow night. Maybe we take it easy the rest of the day?"

Nothing sounded better.

While she buckled her seatbelt, as he shifted into reverse Damien's hand brushed hers. The air snapped blue between them with a static shock. For no sensible reason at all, Ravyn blushed, her mop of hair a shelter for burning cheeks.

Damien, however, simply reversed and drove them back to the inn.

It would be reasonable to assume a person's first night ever in some foreign country would be spent wide-eyed and agog, steeping in the new culture, land and surroundings. But Ravyn's wasn't.

Waking to the sound of ice pebbles hitting the window, a limpid, gray light permeating her room, she had foggy recollections of driving to the top of a small hill in the light of a sunset glow. Of a sign that Damien said read "Fairy's Rest." And of the bungalow itself, only large enough for a handful of guests. It's café, though, judging by the number of diners visible through the warm-lit windows, had been bustling.

Having been enchanted by it when they walked up to the inn, she clearly remembered the charm of a stone walkway that ambled off from the front entrance to circle a pond just large enough for skating, a quaintly rustic sign indicating free skates could be had inside. A small stand of birch at the waters edge was flanked by landscaped bushes, brown remains of summer's fern, and a wooden bench with intricate carvings too detailed to be clearly discerned from a distance.

Inside the bed and breakfast, Ravyn had leaned against the wall, clutching her purse, the rest of her luggage at her feet, waiting as Damien registered them with the desk clerk. A low hum of conversation and the warm smell of food from the café hung in the air. To the side, a small, chair-filled parlor featured a beautiful stone fireplace filled with charred wood speckled white. An evergreen garland was draped across the mantel. Sconces holding unlit candles hung on the walls.

Damien returned, handing her an old-fashioned brass key trimmed with a scarlet ribbon as she did her best to keep her eyes wide open. "Looks like you'll call it an early night?" he said.

With a vague sort of nod, she'd walked up the stairs with him to find their rooms, her stomach grumbling as the aroma of French onion beef stew and baking bread lingered in the short hallway.

Aside from waking once to the muffled sound of a drum, singing and fiddles, the world beyond her door well may have disappeared for all Ravyn knew of it. Until the ice-storm came pelting pebbles of ice against the window panes, bringing her fully back to the world.

Stretching to the tip of her toes, luxuriating in the softly comfortable bed, Ravyn yawned, idly looked about the room in the dim light, marveling at the wonders a short but deep sleep could do to refresh a body.

Not even bothering to sit up in bed, she picked up the handset of the antique European-style phone from the nightstand beside her, cradling it between her ear and shoulder to dial room service. Ordering a small entree with pastries and coffee, it was only after hanging up she realized the entire conversation had been in English.

Even her language app aside, at least she wasn't wholly dependent on Damien in this foreign land.

Content with the quiet light seeping in from behind the drawn curtains and not wanting to disturb the integrity of her somnolent reflections, she stretched again, closed her eyes a moment, then reached for the notebook and pen in her purse. Scribbling words fresh from sleep to describe the immense physicality of the dolmen and its sheer persistence through time, a knock at the door made her jerk. Ravyn's notes scrawled illegibly off the page.

Thinking it was rapid-quick room service, she turned on the lamp switch only to find the power was out. With a grumble, Ravyn grabbed her Tinkerbell bathrobe (bought especially for this trip by a mother whose subtleties of humor were well known to her daughter if few others), bumbling and bumping her way to the door in the low light, stomach skirling soft little growls in anticipation all along the way.

But, door opening, it wasn't room service that waited on the other side. Ravyn swayed backward a step. Damien stood there, backpack casually slung over one shoulder.

"What time is it?" she asked, pulling her bathrobe closer more to cover the Tinkerbell embroidery on the one pocket than anything else.

"A little after five." He smiled. "Sleep well?"

The muffled sounds of singing and guitar music wound their way up the staircase.

"A party, I take it?" She nodded downstairs. "Music? Dancing?" Pressing her lips, she hid a grimace.

"It's the Solstice. And it's France. It's a sure thing it'll be going on all night."

She cocked her head. "I thought the Solstice was tomorrow."

"Yesterday, *that* was when it was tomorrow." He smiled a little.

"Yesterday?" She tucked a stray curl behind her ear. "You mean…?"

"You slept a while."

That explained why things were still light outside even though they'd checked in around sunset. "Power's out in here," she said.

"It's the storm. Power's been coming in bits all day." Digging into his backpack, he held up a rolled cylinder. Its seal, scarlet and embossed, was broken. "We need to talk about this." He shrugged. "But I'll come back later."

Damien turned to leave, but Ravyn stopped him. "It's fine. Come in." She stepped back to let him through. "Where'd you find that thing?"

Before he could answer, and before she could close the door, room service arrived pushing a cart. It held a quaint silver tray, its edges bordered with delicate silverwork. A couple platters sat on prettily trimmed paper doilies next to what looked to be a vintage silver coffee pot, its handle and fluted spigot elegantly sculpted into bas relief patterns of leaves and flowers. "*Merci*," she managed before pushing the cart herself into the room.

Walking past the mirror, Ravyn caught a glimpse of her reflection. "Oh geez." She stopped to grab the brush from her purse, attempting to smooth her unruly mop. "Give me a minute."

Damien pulled a couple candles off the food cart and the holders provided. "Mind if I do a quick sweep of the room?"

"Um." It seemed an odd time for house-cleaning. And why Damien felt compelled to do so seemed, perhaps, even stranger.

"For bugs. You know."

That hardly explained things. "Bugs?" Maybe he had an insect phobia or something.

With a slanted smile, he reached into his pack, pulling out a small device she didn't recognize. "Trevor usually handles things like this, but when he's not here, we do it ourselves."

That made even less sense. "You mean like cockroaches." She'd heard the horror stories of staying in foreign motels. Whether those stories were true or not was another matter.

"Maybe remote controlled ones."

"Remote controlled?" Clearly the conversation was fast slipping away from any sense of shared reality they may have.

"Military grade. You know." He looked at her. "You don't know."

Ravyn slowly shook her head.

"Let's just say that a cockroach controlled by an antenna and a game controller – " He broke off, eyes narrowed as he absently toggled a switch back and forth on the small device he held, a red light flashing on then off as he did so. Voice roughened, he finished, "It's, to be blunt, monstrous."

Even in the dim light, Ravyn could see his cheeks were flushed. After a moment of silence, she asked quietly, "Why? I mean, who would want to do such a thing?"

"The usual suspects. For surveillance. It gives them an edge."

"Mm." It was all she could think to honestly but kindly say before making her way into the bathroom. Ravyn shut the door absently, leaning against it as it closed, feeling a little light-headed. This new position was obviously more complicated than it seemed at first blush. Trevor's presence had said as much, but several thousands miles of travel since then had made what he represented seem more about precaution rather than anything actually necessary.

When she came back out, hair brushed and yesterday's clothes donned, Damien was perched on the corner of the unmade bed, studying something in his hands.

"Any bugs?" she asked, not sure she wanted to know.

Smiling slightly, he shook his head no but then looked over at her, dark eyes serious. "We have a mystery to solve." He let a small tapestry unroll from his hand.

Chapter Eleven

A gust of wind clattered sleet against the window. The candle flames fluttered in the draft that followed. Clearly the storm was still at it.

"You got your cell?" Damien asked. At her nod toward the bureau where it peeked out from the top of her purse, he picked up the phone, placing it in the microwave.

"You going to nuke it?" Only half joking, Ravyn straightened with a partial mind to rise and attempt a rescue mission. "Power's still out."

"Microwaves have a shielding," he muttered, studying the tapestry even as he absently shut the appliance door.

His explanation wasn't particularly helpful.

As he sat down in a chair next to her unmade bed, Ravyn plumped the pillows and smoothed the bed clothes – still a bit embarrassed she'd slept something like twenty-four hours – then sat on a corner, tucking a foot under her other knee as she watched him, waiting.

Interest in what he had to say about the mystery of the tapestry slipped into admiration of his straight, masculine nose, profiled handsomely in the candlelight as he bent his head to study the piece in his hands. Then there was his thick dark hair, long enough to hang just below his shoulders in a rough sort of way. It was pulled back in a man's hasty, low ponytail. A couple streaks of silver caught the low light.

"— don't understand what that means." He finished and looked over at her. "But maybe you have some idea?"

Blanking on their topic of conversation, Ravyn blinked as she met the expectation in his eyes. Then, clearing her throat, she remembered the tapestry. "Can I see it?"

It was a beautiful piece of work, similar to those she'd seen back at MegaLit's HQ. But small. No more than five inches by seven. Its glossy threads, glistening in the wavering light of the candles' small flames, depicted two wolves striding out of a snow-covered forest. An older man walked between them, his gray hair long and free, his beard equally so. Silver threads interlaced both. Gold was sprinkled throughout the fur of the wolves. The old man wore knee-high leather boots over linen-like trousers, his shirt of a similar material. A long brown coat flared dramatically behind him.

But perhaps one of the most telltale aspects of the piece was its border of oak leaves, acorns, and a repeating triad of spiraling circles. "Clearly Druidic symbols, don't you think?" Ravyn traced the border with her index finger. "Where did you say you got this again?"

"I know it sounds strange," he said. "But these tapestries, they're a part of almost all our trips. Like clues. Something to help find the cause of the re-emergence."

"Re-emergence?"

"Of wild magic."

One of these days perhaps she wouldn't need that reminder. Maybe if this whole thing ever, just even once, started to make sense to her. Slowly Ravyn prodded, "And the tapestries come from…?"

He hesitated. "Dreams," he said finally.

"Whose?"

But Damien only dropped his gaze with a small shrug.

When he still didn't elaborate, Ravyn studied the tapestry again, suppressing a flare of annoyance at the layers of secrecy that shrouded so much of the job. "So, this is supposed to help us figure out what's causing the, ah, fairies to, um, return?" She'd managed to say that all with a straight face.

He nodded, eyes intent as he looked at her again. "But these things, they aren't always helpful. Sometimes they're just dead-ends."

Ravyn frowned, suspecting that the questions she had brewing would not get an answer. She simply said, "If we go by this one, I think it's clear there must be wolves here?"

"Not that I know of," Damien said with a shrug. "France doesn't have many wolves. And those it does have, they're in the east, especially the southeast."

"So a wolf returning here could, if I have things sort of right, really spark this 'wild magic.'" She put air-quotes around the phrase. "But where would an animal like that find refuge around the dolmen?"

"Maybe in the Theil, though it seems too small a territory."

Nodding, Ravyn held the cloth so the candlelight flickered across the image. "But it'd make sense. I mean," she corrected herself. "It has a certain logical consistency to it. The dolmen's schist rock probably comes from the

Theil. This connects the two sites. The wolves return to the Theil and then…" Her voice faded. "On second thought, how can that possibly make any logical sense at all?"

Damien's smile was a slow one. "You've got the trick for this. Follow your intution - it's taking you there. Maybe try thinking of the situation like a story. One you're writing. How would you tell it?"

Frowning at the idea but intrigued, Ravyn hesitated only a moment. Then, closing her eyes, fingers arching a little as if preparing to type, she thought it through. "The wolves," she began out loud. "They're like all living beings, carrying their own sort of energy. As wild ones, though, the wolves, they have a special energy." Opening one eye to a slit, she peeked at Damien, fully expecting she was boring him. But instead, his attention was intently on her. Ravyn shifted uncomfortably, closing both eyes again to shut out awareness of a listening world.

With a nervous little cough, she continued. "We all know wolves help out plants and animals physically, but spiritually?" She smiled, getting caught up in the possibilities of the story. "They're a keystone energy, infusing the area with – " She stopped, eyes opening as if to break the spell.

Damien gave an encouraging nod. "With?" he prompted.

"Wild magic," she said, annoyed that the little exercise in fiction had brought about such a concession to Damien's assertions.

Firm and handsome, Damien's lips spread into a broad smile, one that seemed to almost reflect a sort of pride. "You see it."

Folding her arms, she scowled. "I'm not saying I buy it. But, okay, it does have its own strange sort of logic to it. Barely." Eager to be off the slightly unnerving topic, Ravyn swiveled the focus of their conversation a bit. "But I don't get what the guy in the tapestry has to do with anything. A wolf whisperer, maybe?"

Damien shrugged, palms up. "Sounds reasonable.

"Maybe you should ask around. Or we, I mean."

Damien crooked another smile. The flames from the candles cast flitting shadows across his face. "Are you saying you're ready for the Solstice party?"

Ravyn studied the ceiling, the floor, each of the walls in turn as she tried to think of an excuse. "I'd love to," she finally said. "But I haven't showered for a while, thanks to my nap. And the power's out, so, you know, I can't really get ready..."

The lamp, evidently on its brightest setting, suddenly lit the room as the low hum of the room's little fridge filled the small space. *Traitors*, Ravyn thought, glaring at them both in turn.

"Okay, then. Guess that settles that." As if not giving her a chance to say otherwise, Damien rose quickly. "I'll drop by in about an hour, give or take. It'll be good, this party, something to do before we leave for the dolmen. After we'll see if the fairies have any of their own festivities."

"Sure," she said, unable to muster the appropriate enthusiasm, at least not for the party. For the latter, however, she was looking forward to disproving MegaLit's ridiculous theory. Fairies indeed. The Wild Magic Theory, however logical it may be within its own worldview, made no sense at all in the real world.

As Ravyn and Damien walked into the crowded anteroom, people spilling over into the lobby, some evidently recognized Damien, and he smiled a sort of half-smile at them when they called out a greeting, not stopping to talk. Apparently he hadn't wasted time napping as she'd done.

The party was at full tilt. Despite the power being back on, none of the electric lights were. Instead the wall-hung candles flickered in a dazzling array of tiny golden flames. A fire blazed in the fireplace. Music, smells of good food, and general joviality filled the small place. Fiddle music seemed to practically leap about the room as if in an eager romp with the rolling thud of the bohdrán.

The two of them settled against the rear wall. Ravyn folded her arms wishing she could pop into the old-fashioned floral design on the wallpaper.

Damien glanced down at her with a brief smile, folding his arms too as he leaned more firmly against the wall.

They stood that way, silently, for some time. Enough so that the music and the folk dances on the dance floor changed a couple times over.

"You don't dance?" she said eventually by way of making conversation, wondering why he wasn't asking any of the beautiful French women in the room, especially one of those casting eyes at him, to join the dancing. She had to talk loudly to be heard over the music.

Inclining his head so near her own that his hair brushed her cheek, he asked, "You, you're wanting to dance?"

"Me?" Ravyn blinked. "That's, um, that's not – "

But evidently she wasn't getting through. Damien took her by the hand, leading her to where everyone was coalescing into another sort of dance formation. Ravyn's heart sank. Her feet dragged. It was bad enough to get on the dance floor and try to move to a beat on her own. But dancing with someone else? Not to mention staying in time with a whole group of other dancers? This she did not do.

Especially when the dance partner in question was someone like Damien. There was zero chance of getting through with grace.

But it turned out her feet could move on their own, given a chance, at least with the fairly simple steps of a dance that had the men weave through the slowly shuffling women's line.

Which meant Damien wasn't her only partner, nor she his, giving time for short interactions with strangers. The nature of the these, on Ravyn's part at least, consisted of smiling and nodding the like of which provided absolutely no helpful information on La Roche aux Fèes that she was able to discern. She hoped Damien, though, managed to get a question or two in about wolf whisperers hereabouts – in between the flirts and the smiles, that is.

These last were keenly observed by Ravyn. So much so when the dance returned them to each other, she kept her eyes on her feet, holding Damien's hand lightly with only her fingertips.

The song over, both returned to their wall. Neither danced again. Someone brought them slices of *bûche de Noël*. Damien kept her well stocked with Solstice punch, catching various short conversations en route between their table and the punch, mostly with the multitude of women scattered thereabouts. With much leaning in toward each other, smiles, and flutter of women's lashes, these communications clearly went beyond the requisite polite and courteous sociability etiquette demanded.

Not that Ravyn was keeping watch or anything.

But the two of them themselves didn't say much to each other. Except once. "Nobody knows anything about wolves. Not of any around here, anyway," Damien told her. "But they haven't heard reports of any fairies returning either."

Ravyn nodded wanting to note that he'd rarely asked the men. At least not as many, in her estimation. Not quite anyway. Or so it seemed.

It should have been delightful. The music was great. The punch delicious. The people highly convivial.

Yet it seemed ages had already passed when Damien leaned over to whisper in her ear, "I think we've let them crash our party long enough, yeah?" Smiling, his eyes holding hers, he tilted his head to the exit.

Ravyn swallowed, uncomfortably aware of how unprofessional the source of her delight – bubbling like a colorful seltzer – was. The sudden giddiness made her wonder about the punch, and she nodded, glancing up at him as she ducked out into the lobby where they'd stashed their winter gear for the trip to La Roche.

He smiled down at her as she passed.

Calm now that the storm had worn out, the night air was crisp and cool but not bone-chilling as she and Damien made their way out to the car. Despite her doubts regarding the fairy fire, the night wove its own magic, and Ravyn found that part of herself actually half-believed they were on the verge of meeting ethereal beings of legend. "Are you sure there wasn't any alcohol in that punch?" she asked Damien as her feet slipped on the icy walk. She caught hold of his arm to steady herself.

"That's what they said." His cheeks too were flushed.

By the time they reached the car, landing in a tumbled heap on the icy pavement at least three times over, it was clear driving on the slick roads was out of the question. Damien opened the passenger door for Ravyn and she settled on the seat inside. "Be right back." He left without further explanation.

Hip sore from that last landing, Ravyn left the door open, stretching her leg to ease the soreness. Beyond, iced tree limbs glinted like so many tiny diamonds in the moonlit landscape. An almost balmy breeze blew through them.

If there were fairies thereabouts, the setting couldn't have been more fitting.

"Don't let go of that potato!" Damien's call came from behind her a few minutes later, startling Ravyn so she hit her head on the low ceiling of the little car. Wincing, Ravyn glanced around. "Potato?"

With a grin, he brandished two pairs of ice skates. "See? We can still do this."

"Skate there?" Her tone was incredulous. But, reaching for the smaller pair, she pushed off her boots anyway.

Damien stuffed them in a duffle bag along with his own boots for use later.

It was a while since Ravyn was on anything like ice skates. Rollerblading was a little more recent but not recently enough for her comfort. Still, she did fairly well, only falling once on the way out as her feet slid from their moorings while simply standing in place, waiting for Damien to situate his camera gear.

Damien, however, seemed as if he'd been born on skates. Being Québécois, he probably had, Ravyn reflected.

"Play hockey much as a kid?" she asked as he circled back around her another time before sliding into pace beside her. Another patch of sporadic, thin woods hugged the road close. An old home of brown and white stone, crumbling yet picturesque, emerged from the brushy hedgerow.

"Don't all we Québécois?" he asked over the hushed sluicing of their skates.

She wouldn't know.

In the two mile skate along the main road, not another soul intruded on their journey. The wind had died significantly, leaving the ice-sheathed fields to glitter calmly in the moon's glow.

Just before La Roche aux Fées, oaks became more common, their large trunks and bared limbs a change from the smaller brush and trees before. Passing a road sign that marked the parking area just ahead, the road tilted downhill. It was only a slight incline but, given the rough quality of the road ice, it was enough to slow Ravyn to a near crawl.

Or want to.

Unfortunately for them both, Ravyn's skates slid faster than the rest of her could keep up. As she wobbled, Damien reached out and steadied her. Before she could thank him, however, her foot slipped, hit Damien's and they both fell on their backs, laying side by side like pinned insects in someone's treasured collection.

"Ow," Ravyn said eventually.

Damien groaned.

Laying there in silence, the only sound was the oddly musical rustling of the oaks' iced-over branches glittering in the moonlight, sounding more like tiny whisperings than icy clatter.

Damien sat up slowly. "Do you smell that?"

Not sure how to move in a way that wouldn't tear her spine apart, Ravyn lay there sniffing the air. "Woodsmoke?"

Getting to his feet on the ice as gracefully as if he didn't have sharpened blades for foot wear, snow caked into the furrows and creases across the back of his winter coat, Damien peered cautiously through the oak grove that stood between them and La Roche aux Fées.

"I'm going to go take a look," he told her, holding out his hand to help her up.

But Ravyn shook her head, not wanting to knock Damien down again. "I think I'll just lay here another minute or two," she said. "You go ahead."

"You're good?" he asked, frowning a little.

Ravyn nodded.

He didn't go far, just the edge of the road. Not wishing for another fall, Ravyn eased onto her side then to all fours, glad to find her back entirely intact. Scrabbling across the icy road like an overgrown infant to the road's shoulder, she held to a tree there for support while she took again to standing on two feet.

The tree blocked her view of the dolmen, and Ravyn shifted carefully to the other side, peering next to Damien from around its large trunk. Her sudden appearance seemed to startle him, but he gave her a smile and nodded toward the dolmen.

Surrounded by oaks, the mammoth stones stood maybe a hundred feet beyond the two of them. Any passing observer might note the structure was bathed in moonlight and move on.

But neither Damien nor Ravyn had been sent as casual observers.

At first glance, Ravyn felt gratified that her suspicions there was nothing fairy afoot at La Roche were well founded.

Damien, however, stood still. His only sign of movement an escaping mist of breath.

Brows pulling together, Ravyn glanced at him again, then studied the dolmen more closely. It was beautiful there in the moonglow. Ice from the storm, no doubt, had encased the stone making it shine like it did.

Looking back, Ravyn couldn't be sure how her focus shifted as they stood there minute after minute in silence, only the whispery sounds they'd heard earlier softly filling the air. But it did. Gradually she became aware of an ephemeral light bathing the structure from within.

Like staring at a flame for far too long, she narrowed her eyes, sure she imagined the pale shimmer of blue. Moonlight suffused things. It didn't dance like this did. Its shadows didn't flutter about. And it certainly didn't shine with quite that bluish of a hue.

Or did it?

Lips parting, Ravyn's eyes grew dry before she remembered to blink. Breath short, she pushed away from the oak, not entirely sure of her goal.

Chapter Twelve

As Ravyn took a step forward into the snow, one hand on the trunk of the oak as she launched, there was a quiet tug on her sleeve, and she looked over her shoulder.

Damien held up the duffle bag carrying their boots.

She grimaced. Hiking through snow in ice skates wasn't on her list of particular talents. She took a step back toward Damien to change out of her skates.

But this was a mistake.

Ice from the storm had clustered in the space between the roots of the oak tree. As her weight settled on one leg, the blade of the skate slipped smoothly on an icy patch as it was designed to do. Her other foot, however, was mired in snow, and she fell with a crash into a neighboring thicket.

Damien started forward, helping her up. Holding her by the elbow, they both looked to the dolmen, breathing stilled. Even the whispering branches were silent.

The dolmen still shone in the moonlight, but shadows no longer flickered. The light no longer danced. And it certainly wasn't a pale blue but rather a cool white light bathing not only the stone slabs but also the oaks and fields of snow with its suffused glow.

"They're gone, aren't they?" Ravyn whispered.

"Who?"

But she caught Damien's amused smile and hemmed a little as she realized what it was she'd just admitted. "Not that I actually thought…" She couldn't figure a graceful way to reboot her initial question. "Whatever it was, the flicker's gone."

"The fairies, I didn't really think to see them for real," Damien said, unzipping the duffle and handing Ravyn her boots. "But it doesn't mean there aren't any signs. Tracks. Warm embers. Any of these things."

Forgoing her skepticism for a while (not that she actually believed they'd been seeing cavorting fairies or something, not really truly), as she managed to ease one foot out of its skate and into its winter boot, Ravyn pressed, "Don't they kind of have a reputation for being, I don't know, unforgiving of trespass?" On the far off-chance there was something to all this, she wanted to be sure.

Damien nodded. "Ah, but we brought gifts."

"We did?" She drew on her last boot.

But he didn't explain, plunging as he already was into the small woods toward the dolmen. Snugging her small purse-pack crosswise across her torso, Ravyn took a deep breath and followed Damien's lead. Moving swiftly, almost loping, in a half crouch from massive tree trunk to massive trunk, he kept a low profile. Surely if anything magical were about, it would note them both, low profile or no, but she did as he did anyway, exercising extra caution to avoid any further mishaps.

"Where's your camera?" she whispered as quietly as she could when she caught up. Even so it felt as if her voice fairly boomed through the small woods.

"Where I can get it, if I need to." His eyes were trained on the towering stones ahead as they crept lithely forward to the nearest large tree trunk, keeping low.

When they reached the dolmen itself, Damien somehow managed to scuttle to the rear yet still maintain his dignity. Relaxing back against the rock, he sat on his heels watching Ravyn's sly but scurried approach as she scrambled from one tree trunk to the other. Her shoulder brushed his as she settled near him. Damien turned his head at the touch and their eyes met briefly before he slowly raised a finger to his lips.

Ravyn nodded, understanding. Or at least she understood the latter. The tenderness in his eyes had been less fathomable – a reflection, no doubt, from the light of the moon.

Except for the soft hooting of an owl not too far away, all else remained still, almost empty of sound, a silent night. The moon continued to suffuse the landscape in soft white, shafts of its light even penetrating the interior of the dolmen with an eerie glow that illuminated its shadows in ways the sun never could.

Ravyn's calf muscles began to ache from the cramped way they moved slowly along the structure's periphery, their footfalls a soft, nearly synchronized shuffle. It was an age before they reached the entrance. Slowly easing around to the front, Damien straightened and Ravyn rose as well.

The place looked as it had earlier, only cast in the subtle play of moonlight rather than the watery remains of the day. Damien strode into the interior as if certain of what he sought.

Ravyn, however, hovered again at the entrance, unwrapping an energy bar as she scanned the area for signs of anything unusual.

A soft breeze caught at the bar's wrapper, and it fell to the ground at her feet. Absently picking it up to stuff in her pack, she'd found she had also grabbed hold of what she took to be the papery skeleton of a leaf. It fell from her hand. And caught the moonlight, sparking briefly blue before fluttering back to the ground.

Ravyn stared at the area around her feet, shifting them slightly. "Damien," she called a few moments later, her voice calm even as shimmering bits of pale blue defied gravity, rising slowly to float with her movements.

Damien rounded the corner of the dolmen as Ravyn spun slowly, the centerpoint to a swirl of blue dust sparking brightly with her movement. She smiled over at him.

"*C'est incroyable.*"

Ravyn never imagined his gaze might be more on herself than on the eerily beautiful phenomenon happening all around her. "What do you think it is?" As she stopped, the sparks settled too.

For a moment, Damien's gaze remained intent, as if seeing the very last spark through to its last little glimmer. But a crease soon furrowed between his brows and his voice was soft, even controlled, as he said, "Don't move yet, but we may have a problem."

Ravyn looked questions at him, alarmed ones.

"Those could be ashes from a fairy fire," he explained. "The blue embers."

Ravyn narrowed her eyes. "Not really."

He nodded. "And their magic – " He stopped.

After several moments when he didn't continue, Ravyn prompted, "What about it?"

"Their magic, it can be – " Damien looked at her. "Well, we don't really know what we have here. Just don't move."

Ravyn snorted, but softly. "Why? The moment I move I'll fall down a fairy sinkhole or something?"

"Or something," he said, unzipping a side pocket in the duffle bag.

She sighed as she stood still, watching Damien as he pulled a small handful of foil-wrapped candies from the bag, inexplicably scattering them at the base of a large oak tree, half dead by the looks of it, the only tree there protected by a low fence. Hand emptied, he put the flat of his palm against the tree's trunk, eyes lowered, lips moving.

"You're not offering me as a sacrifice or anything, right?" she called to him, more or less certain she was joking.

He didn't answer right away which gave Ravyn's pulse a bit of a kickstart.

"Should I?" he asked, finally walking back to her, a slight smile on his face, hands in his coat pockets. "But maybe they'd prefer the chocolate?" He held out a handful. The foil wrappings caught the soft glow of the moon as he offered them to her.

Biting into some of the most delicious chocolate she'd ever tasted, Ravyn nodded. "The candy's definitely a better bet." Shifting her feet, Ravyn was distracted as more sparks flickered blue in the moonlight. Breaking what felt disconcertingly like a near-trance, she asked, "Can I move now?

With a quick look around, Damien nodded, holding out his hand. Unnecessary as it seemed, Ravyn took it anyway, stepping tentatively out of the ashes (if that's what they really were), half-convinced there was a flurry of wings behind her coming to sweep them both away.

Of course there wasn't.

Still, the hair prickled up the back of her neck. "I think we've seen what we need to see," she said, hoisting her pack in preparation for leaving.

Damien's eyes were soft as they continued to search the woods surrounding them. "You feel it too."

Ravyn shrugged. "Maybe."

"I don't think it's malicious."

Ravyn shrugged again.

"But you'd rather leave anyway?"

Hesitating only briefly, Ravyn nodded.

He took a deep breath. "Probably best. Leave them to do their thing. If we stay we could scare them off for good." Chin lifting, his shoulders relaxed as he watched the forest. "But it's nice to know the fairies, they're back. Even if barely just."

Eyebrows raising, Ravyn made no comment.

By the time they returned to the inn, everything was dark save for the faint glow of a single lamp in the inn's foyer. Only just now finished with the cleanup, the innkeeper greeted the two of them as they came in. "You made it?" he asked in accented English. "All that way, with the skates. You counted the stones?"

Damien's chuckle was weak at best. He glanced at the floor without answering, but Ravyn enthused, "Yep! Earlier. Forty-two exactly."

"You are agreed? You two?" The innkeeper was grinning as he put the broom into a small closet.

Ravyn nodded, a little perplexed by the man's enthusiasm.

Damien busied himself with taking off his skates.

There was time for a couple hours nap before sunrise and the official (human) Solstice bonfire at La Roche, but wired as she was and her internal clock so discombobulated, Ravyn stayed up doing internet research instead. The road crew had been busy during those intervening hours, too, making the roads passable enough to drive to the dolmen just before dawn.

It was still dark. But it was certainly much more crowded than when they were there only hours ago. A small fire, its flames the normal red and orange, danced at the center of a spiral path that lay in a large clearing to the east of the dolmen just behind the visitor center. The layers of ice and snow from yesterday had melted before its warmth creating a ring of damp meadow grass. A table of festive refreshments, including steaming teacups of hot somethings, stood at the entrance to the spiraling path.

Despite the celebratory air and number of talkative, friendly people, the hum of conversation remained subdued. A quietly expectant chord thrummed among the crowd, pulling the disparate group together as they gathered, a long line spiraling in close to the fire, many sipping from the tiny, steaming cups.

But Damien and Ravyn bypassed the throng. The area immediately around the dolmen had only a few scattered visitors, at least human ones. An early rising bird twittered tentatively into the dimness before the dawn, a beautiful singer Damien identified as the European robin. Tree limbs, still iced, held the peachy light of a new morning. As they approached, a chill wind blew through the corridor of the dolmen. The rustle of dried leaves stirred within.

The remains of the fire or whatever it had been that they'd seen last night were gone, presumably swept away by the visitor center attendant tidying things for the special day. Ravyn peered inside the dolmen's gloom. It felt chillier somehow. A freak shaft of dim light glanced off gold wrappings in a corner near the entrance. "*Chocolat Bonnat*," one read.

Never one to tolerate the habits of the common litterbug, as Ravyn reached for the wrapper her attention was arrested by, of all things, a dead plant. Hidden there at the outer edge of the dolmen, just beyond last night's so-called fairy fire, were the unmistakable dried leaves of a starflower clinging to their browned stalk, nestling in a rocky nook, its tiny seed husks held up like an offering to the world.

But it was the chocolate wrappers Damien took notice of. His eyes widened as he too leaned in, arm brushing hers, to pick up the empty wrappers, putting them in his pocket. "Maybe the fairies liked these after all, yeah?"

Ravyn cast him a bemused look as she rose and took a backward step, her heel catching awkwardly on a root from the large oak behind as she did so.

Damien reached out, stopping her fall. His hand remained lightly on her arm.

Ravyn's cheeks warmed. "Jet lag, I guess. It's catching up with me."

Damien nodded toward the Solstice spiral behind them. "*Café viennois* can help with that," he said.

Regarding him with a tinge of suspicion, she asked, only half serious, "That's not like some sort of ceremonial hallucinogen or something, is it? You know, to welcome the Sun and whatnot."

"Hallucinogen?" His face looked blank then he laughed. "Only if you get unusual reactions when chocolate's mixed with espresso."

It was good to hear him laugh. The man smiled a lot, but laughter didn't seem to come as easily.

As they made their way back to the spiral and its refreshment table, Ravyn grinned with her reply, even as she felt a little sheepish. "Not really, no." Unless the hallucination was becoming delusional over the worth of her conversational skills. Caffeine tended to make her chatty. It was probably a good thing this *café*-whatever came in such little mugs. The sugar-sprinkled pastry he handed her at the refreshment table would decidedly not help in that department either. "Start the Solstice with a sugar-high," she said, taking a sip after a quick bite. "Why not."

But Damien frowned. Indeed his own *café viennois* came dangerously close to breaching the lip of its cup as he jerked it up from the table. His eyes, a sudden stormy gray, narrowed as he stared over her shoulder.

Thinking she must have unintentionally but somehow seriously offended a holy rite of French cuisine or maybe the Solstice celebration, Ravyn sipped her coffee. The strength of it made her eyes water, but she took another sip anyway. Nibbling at the pastry, she idly watched the crowd as it slowly (and chattily) wound forward around the fire.

But her eyes soon strayed back to Damien. There was a fierceness to his stare, and Ravyn flinched at first before noting it was apparently reserved for something behind her.

She looked over her shoulder.

A couple was walking toward them, a rather glamorous pair in expensive clothes. As they drew near, Damien's brows came together. "*Que fais-tu ici?*" he said, voice low.

"In English, Damien, please." The woman spoke coolly, her pale eyes icy blue.

Ravyn's attention riveted on Damien. His lips were drawn tight, teeth a thin white line visible between them. Given his usual calm and pleasant demeanor, it was unnerving.

"What." Damien's every word was bit off, edges sharp, as he faced the newcomer. "Are *you* doing here?" He stepped close to Ravyn, arm pressed against hers. She could feel his muscles tense.

Ravyn quickly dropped her gaze, trying to bury her face in the coffee cup. Accustomed to large American mugs, it proved more difficult to do with the tiny thing she held.

"Why, D-man," the woman said, as beautiful as she was cold, slipping her arm through that of the man's she was with, her smile chillier than her eyes. "We have just as much a right to take in all the tourist sites as you."

"You leave this alone, Elinor."

"Still hoping the fairies will turn up?" Elinor continued. "Well, we're here if they do." She patted the arm of the man she was with. "Bianca's not the only one with a bead on these kinds of things, you know."

"Pleasure to make your acquaintance," the man said with a brief incline of his head, eyes all the while fixed on Damien. Face chiseled as a sculptor's work of art, his elegantly trimmed hair was graying at the temples. It accentuated the patrician look of his features.

Damien did not return the sentiment.

"And who's your little friend?" Elinor turned a smile to Ravyn. "Found another one?" But she didn't wait around for Damien's answer. Tightening her grip on her companion's arm, the two strolled away to the dolmen without a backward glance.

That sealed it for Ravyn. An ex. She had to be. The familiarity. The iciness between them. Damien hadn't seemed to be suffering from a broken heart but he was one of those silent ones. Still waters run deep and all that. Ravyn didn't say anything. This was something between the two of them and she'd rather keep it that way.

"*Voici le soleil*," someone said in a low voice, nodding toward the first bright rays cresting the eastern horizon.

Damien slowly drew in a breath while Ravyn drained her *café viennois*, leaving the cup in the washbin as she passed.

As they walked a mauve blush crept across the sky in the east, tinging the fields with a pinkish hue. Although some remained where they were, eyes on the purple and indigo that followed, most made their way to La Roche aux Fées itself, shifting casually into two rough half circles at the entrance to the dolmen, one to the south, the other to the north.

Standing as part of the friendly crowd gathering at the standing stones, Damien whispered in her ear, "We need to get to the Fôret du Theil soon. Very soon."

Ravyn nodded, then looked up at him. "You mean, now?"

He smiled slightly, an expression Ravyn was relieved to see. "Not now." He looked down at her, and from an outsider's perspective it looked as if they both had forgotten all about the Solstice until a small exclamation of delight rippling through the crowd pulled their attention back.

The first rays of the Solstice morning struck the roof of the ice-covered purple schist monument, hitting its mica flakes in a subtle yet dazzling array of light that danced slowly down the rectangular pillars at the entrance. A golden glow crept further down the aisle inside, reaching deeper into the dolmen until it struck the back wall. The entire monument glowed from within, brilliant rays scattered outward through the spaces between the standing stones, tossing sparks of light off the iced trunks and branches of the oaks, both young and old alike.

People started holding hands. Someone began singing, the words in French.

Shifting her feet to dispel the awkwardness as the outsider she felt herself to be, Ravyn watched a robin brave the frosty morning. His weight bent the bough of a tall bush. Watching him nip as he did at the dried fruit there – so like the birds she knew back home – made her feel a little less of a stranger, a little more of just a human doing what so many had done before them. The warmth of the rising sun spread across her face. One Solstice sunrise of thousands.

If only the morning could have melted away on those notes. The camaraderie and beautiful sunrise mixed together into a pleasant atmosphere to which, even as the literal alien among the native-born, Ravyn was not immune.

The acerbic corrective, however, intruded in the end.

Elinor and her man friend pressed through the arc of Solstice celebrants from the other side of the dolmen. Passing Damien and Ravyn, Elinor feigned a dramatic sigh. "So sorry, dear. No fairies this year," she said and continued down the path back to the bonfire and refreshments table with a low chuckle. And a not so friendly glance at Ravyn. Her distinguished gentleman trailed in Elinor's wake, smiling apologetically as he walked by.

Damien pressed a hand to the small of Ravyn's back, gently urging her forward. This time it was not a welcome gesture, but she refrained from protest, too surprised that they were leaving already to do otherwise.

On their way back down the main path, not surprisingly they came nearly abreast of the other two as they stood in the Solstice spiral near the steaming cups of coffee.

"Elinor, you've been warned." Damien's tone was unlike any Ravyn had yet heard from him.

Elinor didn't bother to reply.

Damien pressed Ravyn forward, not taking his hand from her back until they reached the Fiat. He removed it only then to open the passenger door, glancing grimly back down the path they'd just come from. Ravyn wasn't sure he was even aware he'd just propelled her down the path without so much as a by-your-leave.

"Should I ask?" Ravyn began as Damien slid into the driver's seat.

Damien didn't answer, lips pressed together. He turned the key. Quietly, the car's engine started and they rolled smoothly out of the parking lot. Resting his arm on the armrest between them, his braided leather dangled casually from his wrist, the beads shaking slightly with the car's motion. There was a tremble to his fingers too, a tremble that didn't match the movement of the beads. It was so slight Ravyn almost missed it.

"The Market des La Roche aux Fées first and then le Theil?" His eyes remained fixed on the road rolling before them.

"Why the market?"

"Lunch. We might be out there a good while."

"Okay. Sure." Her voice wavered slightly in uncertainty. It was so early, especially, as he himself had told her, for France. And it was a holiday. Most particularly so for Essé. The market might not be open at all. She studied his face in profile. Those narrowed eyes. The slight twitch to a cheek muscle.

Ravyn had been and was willing to play along with the fairy prank, story, outright delusion or whatever it was (although, frankly, it was wearing a bit thin). And she was fine visiting the Theil Forest to see where local folklore said the dolmen's stones had come from. That all fit well with writing what she was sure would be a non-starter of a story about the fairies, but still, it was a rational, appropriate thing to do for the assignment.

But Damien's almost violent urgency to leave, evidently in order get quickly to that forest, made no sense. Nor did its apparent connection to what she continued to assume was his ex-girlfriend. Ravyn looked at him, his jaw still tight. Maybe ex-wife even. It was odd to think of him married. Even formerly married.

In town, Damien parallel parked on the street by the marketplace, turning the engine off. They didn't even have to get out of the car, though, to see it was closed. "You have any food back at your room?" Damien's voice was gentle but tightly wound.

Ravyn nodded.

"Good. You should get it. We could be out there all day."

With that, he started the car again. Hands clenched the steering wheel tightly as he readied to pull out onto the street.

Before he could, however, Ravyn placed a hand – quietly, briefly – over his. "Damien." She said it as a statement not a query. Softly. And waited until he looked over at her. "Is there something going on I don't know about? Something I should."

Dropping her gaze, he remained silent. It was more than a minute or two before he looked at her again. "Elinor came here for a reason."

When he didn't elaborate, Ravyn pressed, "And that would be?"

But his only answer was to give some gas to the car, heading back onto the street.

"Is it Theil Forest?" she asked doggedly.

Turning into the drive of the bed and breakfast, he said simply, "The Theil Forest, she's the first place we planned to look after La Roche. Elinor will figure that out."

Ravyn was intrigued by his assignation of personhood to the forest even as she asked, "Looking for what?"

He glanced at her as if wondering why she didn't remember. "To see if something there caused the Resurgence."

Maybe it was the lack of sleep, or too much *café viennois*, but Ravyn felt a headache coming on. In the parking lot now, Ravyn opened her door.

Damien's hand rested on the handle of his. "I'm sorry for not saying enough about Elinor," he said.

"You don't have to tell me," Ravyn politely interjected. But now he had her almost unbearably curious. If getting in the middle of someone's old love affair wasn't the last thing she wanted to do, she would have pressed to

214

know more. Or at least asked a leading question or two.

"Just…now that she knows." His voice trailed off. "Watch out for her, okay? Elinor's a ghost from the past. A vindictive one. And one I haven't seen in a while." His mouth pressed into a thin line again. "A long while."

"Okay," she said slowly. It certainly wasn't much to go on. Especially when Damien himself was still little more than a stranger to her. Charming, sweet, handsome, and utterly fascinating, yes, but still a huge unknown.

"I'll check with the café. Maybe they're open," Ravyn said, shutting the car door behind her.

But Damien, his eyes closed, steepled fingers pressing against the bridge of his nose, didn't seem to hear.

Chapter Thirteen

Heavy slate clouds arrived mid-day to threaten the sunny promise that had shone across the snowy landscape earlier that Solstice morning. Well-matched with Damien's lowering brow as the day wore on, the cloud bank did no more than lurk along the horizon as if deciding whether or not it was yet a propitious time to strike.

The Theil was turning up nothing but a dead end as far as their particular search was concerned. Gloved hands stuffed in her winter coat, Ravyn kicked at a stone on the shoulder of the narrow road. In addition to any possible (but improbable) sign of wolves, Damien had asked her to look for anything new and unusual as they walked about the woods. But how was she to know what was even normal in this part of the world?

They'd run across a menhir. Ice from yesterday's storm still clung to the rock where it was shaded on the north side. The menhir was unusual, yes, but very well known and definitely not new. Google Earth identified it as Menhir dit la Pierre de Rumfort or "The Strong Man." There was another fallen menhir peeking through the snow just a few feet away, both connected to a celestial alignment of similar stones that had fallen apart over the millennia. Or so web sources said. Local lore disagreed, according to Damien's forays the previous two evenings, arguing instead that the stones had been dropped by fairies en route as they built La Roche.

Either way, it wasn't what Ravyn and Damien needed to find.

Although what, exactly, that was meant to be was still a bit hazy to Ravyn. "If wild magic comes back somewhere, something has to spark it." Damien's voice had been the very essence of kind and gentle patience as he explained the concept, yet again, to Ravyn. "Something it's connected to." He picked up a stone, rolling it between his fingers before letting it drop. "A lot of times, this connection, it's an animal coming back, one driven out decades ago. Or a native plant, one that hasn't been seen for centuries."

She'd scoured the roadside, peeped into the forest, ambled along the fairy's rock-strewn path, cataloging the different brown and shriveled plants she could identify at this time of year. Or at least those she was able to connect to a known American counterpart. Truth was even in the green seasons there would likely be a lot of plants that looked unusual to her in this part of the world – it didn't seem likely she'd know a rare plant for Brittany when she saw it even in all the greenly unfurled glory of summer.

Though she knew she'd have even less success recognizing a rare member of the fauna community, she did keep an eye on the tracks in the snow – but saw nothing more unusual then an occasional squirrel or unknown species of bird.

"Maybe it hasn't returned." Ravyn kicked again at the semi-frozen gravel along the road's shoulder. "The wild magic, I mean." A tiny avalanche of little pebbles rumbled into the bare alder bushes lining the small creek that ran along the road. A faint skin of ice struggled to cover its surface, succeeding faintly only in the slow eddies of shadowed nooks. "After all, we haven't exactly seen any fairies yet." The words sounded silly as soon as she said them. Of course they hadn't seen any.

"I wouldn't say that," Damien replied softly.

"Too bad last night people didn't have more to share," she continued.

"Folks shared things. Interesting things." He shoved his hands in the front pockets of his jeans. His breath, condensing in small clouds, briefly caught the light of a cold sun as he spoke. "Just not things we were looking for."

"There's one thing I don't get." Just one? Ravyn thought even as she said it. But this was one thing she hadn't paid as much attention to at the time as she should have, being distracted as she was with other concerns. "At the Solstice dance, you said people around here hadn't heard of reports of fairies returning. So how could Bianca have heard anything? I thought there must at least have been some odd clip in the news or something."

Damien looked at her briefly before studying a lone patch of green moss on the ground. "Her usual tip."

"From?"

He shrugged. "It's rarely wrong." Sitting back on his heels, a small crease etched between his brows, Damien absently prodded the ground with a broken stick as if looking for the tracks of tiny beings in the miniature fronds of snow-dusted moss.

His evasion didn't escape her notice.

Continuing to poke at the moss, he asked, "Last night in your research, did you see anything about a new wilderness area around here? Or something like that?"

Ravyn shook her head, covering a small yawn instigated by the reminder that she'd spent the wee hours after their midnight run to La Roche browsing the web rather than sleeping. "I'm not sure there's any old growth around here to protect. It looked like the nearest might be almost an hour away. Merlin's Forest or some other name I can't pronounce."

"Brocéliande." He nodded vaguely. "Up by Paimpont."

"The same kind of rock is found up there too," she added. "Merlin's Tomb is made of it."

Ravyn didn't mention that the schist stone La Roche was made of – and so too the Theil Forest menhir – contained a mica crystal believed to provide protection, block certain electronic signals, and even enhance psychic abilities. Damien most certainly didn't need any encouragement in the "woo-woo" direction. Besides, if he could practice evasive conversational techniques, so could she.

Ravyn half-smiled. "But it turns out Merlin's burial dolmen was created a few thousand years *before* he was said to exist."

Damien evidently failed to appreciate the irony. "Merlin. And the same stone as La Roche." His eyes caught hers. "In Brocéliande?"

Ravyn nodded. "But the schist is found in other places too," she assured him. "Closer to here than that it is."

Damien nodded slightly, lower lip jutting. "We should probably go see them. The wolf clue in the tapestry might help us narrow down on a location. Maybe there were some in Brittany, somewhere, recent wolf sightings or something? Try the Brocéliande. It's probably one of the largest forests in Brittany. A much better place than here for wolves."

"Guess I didn't have to worry about Elinor getting here before us." As soon as she'd said it, Ravyn wished she hadn't.

Damien's look was sharp, his eyes traveling swiftly to her own. "If Elinor's not here, she's probably already a step ahead of us." With a sudden violence that made Ravyn jump, Damien kicked at the Fiat's front tire. It was just a short kick, but a small spurt of powdery snow rose from the impact. "*Maudit!*"

Though strident, his voice remained quiet, even with that last comment. His tone more than sufficient to convey his meaning, Ravyn certainly was not going to ask for a translation.

Abruptly swinging the car door open, he asked, "Ready?"

Raising her eyebrows at the sharp edge to his voice, Ravyn nonetheless got into the car without comment. Her nose was getting cold anyway.

Back at the inn, he wasn't exactly what Ravyn would call communicative, simply brushing past the door to her room as he went silently into his. She only went into hers when Damien's door clicked softly shut.

Hours later, making her way down to the cafe to do a quick take-out order for supper, Ravyn was surprised to find Damien at a table set for two. Holly ringed a tapered candle as a centerpiece. The small flame flickered. A soft smile lit his face when he saw her. "Super," he said, rising to pull the empty chair for her to sit in. "I hoped you'd come down for dinner soon."

"You could have just knocked," she said, eyebrow quirked. She felt a little underdressed in her favorite cardigan and jeans, comfort-clothes donned solely for a few hours of web surfing as she looked for wolf sightings.

Not wanting to ask for Damien's help all the time, she did her best to translate the menu, but her eyes kept wandering over the top of the menu to watch him. It wasn't because she enjoyed taking sneak peeks when he was unawares (although, admittedly, she didn't hate it), but in the few minutes she'd been sitting there Damien had been ceaselessly in motion. Not anything major. Just little things. Like stirring his ice water with a fork. Folding and refolding the cloth napkin. Finally, Ravyn put the menu down, too distracted to feel confident enough in her translation to eat whatever she'd find on the plate brought to her. "Order for me?" she asked him. "I'm hoping for something like chicken with veggies."

"Surprises, do you like them?" he asked Ravyn, watching her over the rim of his glass as he took a drink of his water.

Ravyn shrugged. "Nice ones, I suppose. Why?"

"Just wondering."

Which likely meant she was getting French Surprise for dinner. Then it occurred to her it might mean he had something for her for Christmas. So she'd have some shopping to do. Would they be back to the States in time?

As if changing tack Damien told her, "So," he began. "There are a few days here that I have to be gone."

"Gone?" She thought their plane left tomorrow anyway.

Slowly twirling the butter knife, he looked down. "Bianca wants us to stay longer. Figure this thing out before we leave France."

"Oh." It would be her first Christmas away from family. She hadn't anticipated that. Part of her rebelled. "And you'll be gone?"

He grimaced, nodding. "Just for a couple days."

"And what about Elinor? I thought there was some urgency with her." And in a way that Ravyn still wasn't all that clear about.

A muscle twitched slightly as his jaw clenched, but he only shook his head. "That, it will get taken care of." He prodded roughly at his salad but gave no further explanation. "But I have a surprise for you. A good one," he said, eyes kind as they met hers. "It should set things right."

Ravyn held his gaze at first, but, eyelids fluttering in a wholly involuntary reaction as her defiance melted away, she dropped it soon after. "Alright," she said quietly, irked at her own meekness.

There wasn't much else to say during the fairly subdued dinner (at least subdued on Ravyn's part), except, perhaps, to mention that the chicken was delicious.

And that neither had found a report about the return of wolves to Brittany.

The tapestry of the old man and the wolves, then, seemed to offer little in regards to clues.

Chapter Fourteen

Damien's mysterious need to leave Essé evidently didn't start until the early morning of December 23. That left them one day to sleuth out any remaining presence of wild magic at La Roche or causes for it in the vicinity.

Except for several more enjoyable walks together, however, they didn't find a thing. Not even a stray ethereal blue spark floating about the grounds at La Roche as they searched the woods and surrounding lawn, even stepping illegally across the fence to briefly investigate the neighboring vineyard.

None of this surprised Ravyn, but Damien seemed to take it to heart, burrowing his nose in the collar of his coat as a chill wind swept across the field. The sun itself made little effort to appear in the cloudy sky.

Despite these disappointments and even when Damien did indeed depart, it must be said Christmas in France held a certain appeal for Ravyn. And there were still holiday errands to run, perhaps made all the more urgent at missing those family members as the big day neared. The season still carried its anticipatory excitement albeit with a twist.

Snow dusted Ravyn's curls as she made her way down the Rue des Fées late afternoon the day before Christmas Eve, walking solo to the market in the heart of downtown. She was intent on looking for some gifts and stocking up on food for when the shops would be closed over the holiday.

Storefront windows sported electric candles, the flicker of their golden flames almost as cheery as if they were real. Miniature winter dioramas, their blankets of faux snow and cozy lit villages dotted with miniature white-trimmed fir trees, were common among the window displays. Damien was conspicuously absent, and Ravyn felt it even as she mentally repeated the key French phrases she'd asked him to teach her so she could explore the town while he attended to his long distance errand. Whatever this latter might be, he'd remained cagey about it.

Pausing with her hand on the knob of the door to Au Marché aux Fées, its large glass panel plastered with posters, Ravyn worried, again, that without Damien she was likely to say the wrong thing. Maybe she'd ask for where she could find the rabbit instead of the bread or something equally stupid. Then she noted there were actually two posters on the door she could, if not outright read, at least make sense of. One was a promo for the Solstice gathering this past Friday at La Roche aux Fées. The second advertised specials featuring burgers with fries.

Before this could boost her confidence much, however, she caught sight of a figure inside wearing a fine dress coat, gray scarf tucked neatly under the coat lapels. He strolled down the aisle directly in front of the shop's entrance. With his cleanly shaven and chiseled features along with a trimly masculine haircut, gray gracing his temples, there could be no mistaking the elegant man who had been with Elinor at La Roche. It was odd how comforting his face was, though it was only remotely familiar and that familiarity itself derived from a hostile encounter.

With a deep breath, Ravyn pushed open the door, a small chime tinkling to announce her entrance. The market smelled of varnished wood and warm bread, fried onions, and some other delicious aroma Ravyn couldn't place. Her mouth watered.

The man looked up as she walked in, raising a black-gloved hand in greeting, features softening into a smile as if they were old acquaintances already. Ravyn nodded and, unsure where to go next, found herself rather rooted to the spot just as she had been moments before on the other side of the door. Elinor's friend came forward, smile still on his face, eyes on her since she'd entered the store.

"Picking up snacks for the trip home?" he asked pleasantly, shifting the market basket he carried in one hand to the other.

With the amiability of his greeting, Ravyn's heart warmed toward him. "Well, actually, we're not heading home right away."

"Oh?" The sharpness in that one word made Ravyn jerk her head up. Her eyes caught his. They were friendly enough as he asked, "Staying for the holiday then? Christmas in France. Sounds romantic."

"No, we're not – that is…it's that…" Nothing about the man made her hesitate but Damien's reaction to Elinor in the days prior gave pause to her words. "Yes," she found herself saying. "Christmas in France." She put on a cheery smile. "Can't pass that up!"

A presumptive knowingness lit his eyes but he kept them hooded. "Leaving for home afterwards then? Or taking in the sights more?"

The wariness she felt Damien would expect of her kept her answer vague. "We'll probably take in the sights as we make the trip home."

"After the holiday, maybe? Two nights from now?" he asked with another charming smile. When no answer was forthcoming, he prodded, "If so, we might share a flight back to the States."

Thinking how one of her heroines might react to such a prodding from someone who had questionable acquaintances like Elinor, Ravyn, intently studying the market baskets within arm's reach as if her choice of which would carry her groceries held great import, merely commented, "That would make for an interesting trip." She was fully aware such a flight with Elinor and Damien both aboard would be an uncomfortable one indeed.

The man's face reddened slightly but he continued. "No family back home who'll be missing you over the holidays?"

It was a peculiarly too-familiar question for her taste. Or maybe she was simply getting caught up in the part. Cocking her head, she only asked, "Do you?"

His blue eyes widened faintly. "A wife and three girls," he said.

It was her turn to be surprised. "So Elinor isn't…" Her voice trailed off as if embarrassed its operator had had the temerity to speculate on such a thing about a stranger.

"Elinor?" The man smirked. "I'm her boss." As if that explained away everything.

Funny how a situation could get awkward so quickly.

There wasn't much to add after that, although Ravyn now had several questions she would have liked to ask. Such as, if he was Elinor's boss, what kind of work did they do that would bring them to La Roche aux Fées? Mumbling something about having a good holiday, she took a basket and made her way deeper into the aisles of the food market, not at all sorry she'd been guarded with her answers.

Maybe Damien wasn't simply overly paranoid about an old girlfriend. Maybe there actually were others out there trying to scoop the story. The totally non-story story, as it was (not so suprisingly) turning out.

The snow was falling heavier by the time Ravyn made it back to the inn. A line of snow trekked past the registration desk melting beneath the evergreen garland draped across the front of it. A small fiber optic Christmas tree slowly changed color beside the guest registry. It was turning a deep shade of red when the inn keeper stopped Ravyn to give her a phone number. "Anything you need for the holiday, you call me," he said handing her a paper with a number written on it. "Any time. My wife or me, we are here if you need something."

"*Merci*," Ravyn said. She looked at the slip of paper he handed her, a small crease forming between her brows. "The front desk is closed then tomorrow?"

"*Oui, mademoiselle*. But my wife or me, we are happy to help if you need. You call, no problem." His cheeks were a round and cheery red as he smiled.

Ravyn folded the small piece of paper, slipping it in her coat pocket as she absently followed the snowy trail across the red carpet and up the stairs. It was only when the tracks turned, stopping at her door, that they begged for and caught her attention. Shifting the weight of the burgeoning cloth bags so as to carry both in one hand, she looked back down the hall, studying the boot prints. They all traveled in the same direction. Someone had stood outside her room. But they hadn't left. Not in snowy boots anyway.

Carefully sidestepping the threshold to her door, she took the additional two steps needed to get to Damien's and knocked softly. "Damien?" she called, hoping somehow he'd returned.

But no one answered.

Eyeing the boot tracks at her door again, noting snow was visible beneath the door's bottom edge, Ravyn swallowed and knocked on Damien's again, daring to knock louder this time.

Still no answer.

Then she heard a faint click as of a deadbolt sliding open.

She straightened, looking hopefully at the knob to his door, willing it to turn.

Instead her own opened.

Before she could leap into some sort of defensive posture, the bags from the market being a significant hindrance to quick reflexes, the faces of her mom and dad peered through the doorway. Her mom's black curls, so similar to her own, seemed to bounce of their own accord as her mother fairly danced in place, hands clasped, grin wide.

"Hey, honey." The delight in her dad's grin gave stiff competition to her mother's, his deep blue eyes glowing almost as if lit with that elusive fairy fire.

"What are you – How did you – ?" Ravyn couldn't quite complete a thought. Nearly dropping her bags, just in time she thought to place them carefully on the floor before embracing the two of them at once. As she did so, she saw Damien sitting inside, hands clasped loosely between his knees.

"Damien arranged it," Ravyn's mother said.

In the room, Damien's gaze dropped to the floor, the toe of his boot smudging out a clump of snow that hadn't yet melted. But he glanced up again and caught Ravyn looking at him.

She smiled at him over her father's shoulder before stepping back just in time to stop an unwrapped Christmas package from falling out of one of the bags.

Looking around, the older version of Ravyn clasped her hands more tightly together. "Can you believe it? Christmas in France!" Her cheeks glowed warmly. "And I'm starved. Anyone else starved? We should have dinner. Damien, you must be too."

"*Merci,* but you all go ahead."

"Nonsense," she replied. "We won't get to see you over the next couple of days, eh? You're having dinner with us."

"Not get to see you?" Ravyn echoed.

"He's got someone to meet for the holiday," her mom said, not so *sotto voce.*

Damien flushed, clapped his hands on his knees, and stood but without looking at Ravyn. "I should pack," he said.

"Not even time for a bite?" Ravyn's mom pouted slightly through her smile.

At Damien's hesitation, her dad stepped in. "We insist. Our treat."

With a brief look at Ravyn, her eyes still wide with curiosity and maybe a little something else she hadn't thought to identify, Damien nodded.

That evening, Neeja's expressive face morphed through a range of rounding lips and rounder eyes as her clear delight in the proximity of her daughter to such a man as

Damien – and in a locale as romantic as France, no less – shone through. From shifting significant glances during dinner between the two in question (usually only when Ravyn could see) to marveling at the beauty of the small village cozy in the evening glow of snowfall, Neeja took it all in. And she ooh'ed with particular frequency, silently and otherwise (to her credit usually in silence), over every courtesy or kindness Damien showed. These last especially happened so often Ravyn quickly learned to pretend she was unaware of her mother's quiet jubiliations that night.

Ravyn's dad missed most of his wife's significant looks at dinner. But that was because he and Damien were engrossed in a conversation about the "what-ifs" of history, something out of which Samuel had made a career in speculative fiction.

Evidently Damien too had a bit of a background in this line of thinking.

When the two of them got onto the question of what might have been if Columbus had never landed, Damien suggested that the Irish may have already been in contact with the so-called New World given that, long before Columbus sailed, people in Ireland already knew of a land far beyond the sea. This set Sam to wool-gathering, giving Neeja some time to pull Damien into a conversation of her own. It was one that involved a great deal of bragging about Ravyn as a homemaker including her baking skills (more than a little exaggerated) and adroit ability to fashion a comfortable ambience out of nearly any setting.

"Good to know," Damien said breaking off a piece of his dinner roll as he smiled at Ravyn who, cheeks redder than the ketchup she missed on her steak, suddenly became quite certain she'd dropped an earring under the table.

Through no fault of his own, it was almost with a breath of relief that Ravyn found herself about an hour later wishing Damien safe travels. The relief buried whatever sense of abandonment she might feel at his sudden second departure in a wholly foreign country.

He left without much more of an explanation other than that he'd be back after the holiday and the assurance that he'd checked and double-checked that the innkeeper was able to help with anything they might need. Even on Christmas Day.

Ravyn's dad did his best to assure him they'd be fine. "I took some French in high school," he said. "So I know *un poquito*."

"That's Spanish, Samuel," his wife reminded him gently, a smile teasing at the corner of her mouth.

"Right. Well, I took a little of that too, so we're all set."

Neeja slipped a hand through Sam's arm, patting it as she told Damien, "As you can see, we're in good hands."

Chapter Fifteen

Christmas Day dawned beautiful. A lavender-pink sunrise. Light snowfall, just enough to add a freshness to the thin layer already on the ground. But the inn was so empty with folks home for the holidays it would have seemed quite cheerless if it weren't for her mom and dad there to share the day with her. That is once Ravyn and her father were able to extricate Neej from the engrossing conversation she was having with the innkeeper's wife about the flower gardens the inn boasted in the warmer months. Accustomed to Neeja's lifelong hobby, Ravyn and her dad knew it wouldn't be long before seed packets were out and pots planted if the conversation wasn't, ahem, nipped in the bud. They held her winter boots at the ready, proffering them at what seemed propitious pauses in the conversation. Eventually she noticed. Father and daughter were prepared for a rapid extrication.

Determined not to stay stuck inside Christmas Day when all of France remained to be explored yet lacking wheels, with businesses closed for the holiday La Roche seemed a fitting choice, a decision Sam backed enthusiastically, eager as he was to delve into the millennia-old history there. Despite the two-mile walk, soon Ravyn and her mom were strolling about the grounds of La Roche aux Fées while Samuel slowly worked his way to the dolmen itself, peering into each thing that caught his interest. As he explored the dolmen's every nook and cranny accessible to man or woman, mother and daughter sauntered through the trees and fields surrounding it. Their boots creaked on the snow as it glittered in the sun.

"Found any fairies yet?" her mother asked.

"If you ask Damien, he's more than half-convinced we have." Ravyn's wry smile was all the dismissal she need give on the topic. "It does make it somewhat difficult to ferret out a story, though. I don't have much to go on."

"You could write a romance about it."

"Yeah. The place certainly begs for it in some ways. But my boss wants it to be truth-based."

"With a romance? It could be, you know. If you let it." At Ravyn's look, though, her mom moved on, only crooking an eyebrow. "So you're not yet convinced of the existence of actual fairies, hm?"

Ravyn shrugged, though if truth be told, she'd been almost tempted by the magic of the winter's forest sparkling in that starry, moonlit night. It had certainly led her to the threshold of belief, one in which a world of ethereal creatures flickered just beyond a protective veil.

But a threshold is something from which a person can turn back.

Even though the place had grown somewhat familiar to her, the strangeness worn away and the initial shock of the grandness dulled, there was still a presence to be felt there. One that seemed to almost revel in daring her to deny its truth.

The wind, despite the snow, was warm as it blew across the fields, scattering small flurries in its awake.

"Not to intrude into a delicate area, sweetie."

Ravyn braced herself. She knew that tone. And that introductory prelude. "Unsolicited advice ahead?"

"That's what moms are for, right?" She slipped her arm through her daughter's, giving it a squeeze as she did so. "But," she continued, lowering her voice as if the nearby trees and bushes might be pruriently tuning in. "I have to point out you have one very nice, very handsome co-worker. You aren't squandering your time together, are you?"

"Squandering?" Although she feigned ignorance, she knew very well exactly what her mother meant. Ravyn just liked to make her say it out loud as if gathering solid evidence of her meddling. It wasn't the first time the mother had felt her rather shy and quiet daughter might need to be urged into cultivating a matrimonial future.

Before she could answer the actual question, however, Neeja gave her a sharp look. "He's not rich, is he?"

"No, Mom," Ravyn said even as she considered the question. If Damien hadn't been wealthy before MegaLit, with the salaries they paid he could very well be by now.

"Because you know how I feel about dating wealthy men."

"I do." And, after an experience or two, she was no longer inclined to argue. She opened her mouth to argue about this particular situation in question, however, but her mom was quicker.

"Don't date a man with money," Neej reiterated. "Because – "

"He'll just think you're social climbing. I got that, Mom."

"And," her mom said very firmly. "He himself will only be out for a good time. Unless you yourself also, of course, happen to have a million bucks in your backpocket."

"You really think Damien seems like that kind of a guy?" Ravyn's question was serious. Her mother's opinion mattered on this one. "Whatever his economic status."

Neeja's face softened. "No, honey, I don't. But let's just hope he doesn't have a billion dollars banging around somewhere. It'll only ruin a good thing." She patted Ravyn's hand. "Though you know I absolutely do not mean to pressure you, age can creep up on us. And, well, hon, you're past thirty."

"Not much."

"Yeah, well, still past." She looked at her daughter, coming to a stop as she turned to face Ravyn. "And as beautiful as ever, I might add."

Ravyn blushed, gaze dropping to the ground. Mirrors and mothers could be equally embarrassing even as both told her differing stories.

Finger briefly tracing her daughter's cheek, she only said, "Don't for a minute think you see yourself as you really are."

"Hey! You have to see this." Samuel walked quickly their way, hands cupped in front, eyes fixed on what he held. As he strode the last few yards to them, Neeja wrapped up her thoughts for Ravyn, "Just saying. Damien's a keeper. I can tell."

"Mo-om," Ravyn whispered, not sure why she was whispering. "Even if I was, you know, interested – " At her mother's pleased look, she quickly amended. "Which I'm not. He's not here now anyway, is he? Apparently he's taken."

"I don't see a ring on his finger," Neeja sang softly, wiggling her own left hand with its understated but beautifully bedecked ring finger. As Samuel reached them, still oblivious to all else but what he so gingerly carried, she turned her attention to him. "And what has you all in a dither, dear-heart?" Neej asked her husband.

"Look!" Drawing a breath, he held it as he pinched a thin, irregular flake of translucent blue, no larger than a rose petal, from his palm. It shimmered as he held it to the sun, his eyes lit with the same fire as he stared at them. "Now watch." With a short expulsion of breath, he blew on it. It rose briefly as so much sparkling dust before melting away completely, each speck winking away as a tiny blue spark. Pride shone in his grin as if he'd discovered a fairy himself. "It's all along the edges of the dolmen inside."

Surprised into silence, Ravyn moved swiftly back to the dolmen, the hurried footsteps of her parents behind.

Breath shallow, Ravyn rested a hand on the shaped stone in the interior of the entryway, its coolness calming her pulse. The sun warmed her back as she peered inside. The darkness there was again gently broken by slices of light falling through the vertical spacing between the stone giants this time along the western wall. The lichen and moss, in various shades of green, were visible in the dim light, tracing cracks and ridges in the stone until they reached into even the darkest corners.

A soft gust blew in behind her, lingering around Ravyn's ankles before stirring the leaves collected at the bottom of the stone wall. Then, like strange kindling catching spark, a thin brilliance of ephemeral blue traced the path of the winter's wind, briefly illuminating the dark intersection of standing stone and leaf-strewn dirt.

Settling back on her heels, Ravyn sifted the detritus of various autumns through her fingers. Caught between grains of soil and bits of leaf, flecks of blue light flickered, bursting like tiny bubbles until all she held was a dulled handful of dirt.

It didn't seem possible Damien was onto something.

Folding her arms she rested her head against the cold stone. A vague memory from decades ago teased her with its similarities to La Roche. A cool day in northern Michigan, this one in autumn. Skies a solid gray. A Great Lakes fog lifting from Lake Huron – or maybe Lake Michigan – likely both – sifted into the forest as if nothing remained beyond the blurred, soft edges of its realm. Walking through the mist-grayed wonder of a dog-hair aspen stand, the saplings crowding close, it was as if no one else existed in the world. Just her own small family. And the aspen which seemed to go on forever.

A small lake, half-surrounded by rocky cliffs, had lain ahead. Spring-fed, her dad said. On its shoreline, hidden beneath a tangle of autumn-browned grasses below the cliffs, was the lichen-encrusted pictograph her dad had taken them there to see. She couldn't even remember now exactly what the pictograph had looked like. But she did remember how, suddenly, it felt as if the past and present were one. Everything simply was. No end, no beginning. No now, before, or after.

"How curious. What's this doing here?"

Her mother's voice, soft but close behind, startled Ravyn and she turned with a jerk, dropping her small handful of leaf bits and soil.

Crouched, Neeja peered into the small tumbling of rocks at the outer edge of the dolmen where the dried starflower held fast. It was next to what someone – no names mentioned – had claimed not so long ago were the remains of a fairy fire. Tiny glitterings of blue on the flower's browned leaves shone faintly as Ravyn knelt beside her mother.

"That shouldn't be here, should it?" It had seemed out of place when she'd found it the night of the Solstice.

"*Lysimachia borealis*? Not at all. It only grows, or at least is only native to, where we live. Then again, they've always been a special flower for you." She looked over at Ravyn. "Could be it's telling you this new job has you on the right path."

"It's the same job, Mom," Ravyn said dryly. "Just different parameters."

"I'd say. From being in your garret all day to traipsing around the world." Neej stood up, putting a palm solidly on the stone before her.

Ravyn frowned. "Maybe it's saying I shouldn't be here. The dulled flower, at winter's edge, out of place."

Neeja sighed. "She gets that melodrama from you," she told her husband who was examining the exterior of the dolmen now, apparently lost in admiring the contours of the stones. He looked up as if surprised to find others were around, even though he'd been the one to call them over.

"There's some here, too," he said as a response. Licking his finger, he swiped it across one of the cracks in the rock and held it out. "See?" Like a strange mica, the blue dust twinkled briefly in the sun then disappeared.

A mystery substance that crumbled when handled, if a person happened to see it at all. An out of place starflower. A flickering blue in the Solstice moonlight that disappeared when they   approached. "There has to be something we're missing. Something rational, I mean." Ravyn looked around as if the answer lurked in the lengthening of the day's shadows.

"I've not seen anything like it." But her dad didn't seem all that bothered about any need to find a conventional explanation.

Walking around the structure, looking for more of the blue dust her husband had found, Neej called back to them, "Did you and Damien count the stones?"

Ravyn laughed. "It does feel kind of like you have to, doesn't it? Like popping bubble wrap."

Neeja shrugged. "I don't feel the compulsion. Then again, I'm happily married."

Trust her mother to figure out a way to bring that back into the conversation. "Right. Anyway." Ravyn ambled over to her father who was now sitting on his heels, back to the dolmen, watching a small flock of birds fly between the oaks.

Not about to let the matter drop so easily, from the far end of the dolmen Neeja's voice, though muffled by the stones, carried clearly enough. "It's said engaged couples seek the advice of the fairies here, and one way they learn whether they're compatible is if they count the same number of stones." Rounding the corner where she could see her husband and daughter, Neej looked at Ravyn significantly. "Did you?"

Ravyn was not going to give her the satisfaction of saying yes. "That is so made up, Mom."

"You didn't find it in your research?"

It was familiar, vaguely, now that she thought of it. But Ravyn had been more focused on searching out any reported fairy appearances rather than examining the local superstitions regarding romance and counting rocks. Although it would make a great angle. If she was writing a romance about the place. A purely fictional account, that is.

"You should count them now," Neeja continued. "Then we'll get Damien to count them when he comes back. Or bring the two of you out together. Actually, that's probably best." She turned to her husband, ready to ask his opinion.

"Anyone hungry?" Ravyn quickly asked by way of diversion.

Thanks to her father, having never much outgrown his teenaged-boy stage when it came to hunger (nor his simultaneous ability to keep the pounds off), the attempted diversion was a success. Given the general trajectory La Roche kept inspiring in the conversation (or at least in her mother's conversation), Ravyn felt few qualms at urging them back to the inn.

Damien returned the next day, a happy secret seeming to hover at the corners of his mouth. Curious beyond a reasonable measure, Ravyn didn't ask for, and Damien didn't volunteer, any further explanation of his travels.

Unfortunately, the mystery only helped nurture the impact of her mother's advice. Unbidden and resisted, like knapweed infesting a wild prairie Neeja's words slowly bloomed at the back of Ravyn's mind. The result was far from what her mother had hoped, however, as it served to cool Ravyn's interactions with her new co-worker. It may be why she kept her most recent experience at La Roche with its odd blue phenomenon – and out of place wildflower – to herself.

And forgot to mention her run-in with Elinor's boss.

If secrets were to be held, she wouldn't be shy about keeping ones of her own. Even if they were, no doubt, directly pertinent to the project they were working on...as partners. Work-related, that is. Simply business.

Though she did feel a bit guilty about not mentioning the starflower. But Damien had said the *return* of plants could be a catalyst for wild magic, not the introduction of new ones. Besides it had always been, as her mom had said, a special flower in her life, a matter of note she didn't exactly feel like sharing right now.

Chapter Sixteen

Damien came to her room that night – or rather, her doorway. After a brief peek through the peephole at his knock and a glance down at her pink kitty pajama pants, Ravyn did a quick smooth-down of her matching kitten top (as if wrinkles would mar the fashion-effect) and opened the door.

"We have to talk," he told her hovering there on the threshold, backpack in his hand. He didn't seem to notice her casual attire.

"Okay." Ravyn stepped aside to let him in.

Darting a sideways look at her parents' room next door, he asked, "Care for a walk?"

It wasn't a strange request. But Ravyn had caught his look.

Damien's face reddened.

She blinked. "In my pjs?"

He stuffed his hands into his coat pockets, clearing his throat, apparently having found a sudden absorbing interest in the carpet at his feet. "A walk, it might be, ah…" He glanced at her parents' door again before returning to a study of the carpet. "Less of an impropriety."

"Impropriety?" The quaint word was strange between them. "Why would they think anything of it?"

Damien shrugged but didn't look up, instead scuffing his boot against a line in the carpet's elegantly elaborate pattern.

The thought that maybe he'd picked up on her mother's not-so-subtle cues in regards to the matrimonial ideas she had for her only daughter stilled Ravyn's breathing for a moment. After a brief, futile scrutiny of his stubbled and somewhat windburned face, Ravyn frowned but grabbed her winter boots and jacket figuring there couldn't be many people out at this hour. And if there were, surely warm fleece kitten pajama pants weren't the strangest thing they were bound to see in their lives.

He was gracious and courteous as usual, holding doors and letting her through first, but he was silent. It wasn't until they were well along a footpath that led into a small woods, moonlight slanting through the trees leaving slender shadows behind, that Damien gave any indication of what was on his mind. Stopping at a wooden bench, he offered Ravyn a seat at one end, seating himself beside her, knee resting against hers as he put his backpack on the ground and unzipped it. "Take a look at this again," he said, handing her the rolled tapestry. "What do you see?"

Ravyn gently unrolled it, the gold and silver threads glinting in the moonlight. It looked the same as before but she studied it carefully, looking for hidden elements, shifting it in the moonlight the better to clearly see details. "I still just see the old man and two wolves. Trees. Snow." She tried to look even harder, but Damien was already nodding in a satisfied way.

"And the old man, who does he look like?" he asked, eyes intent on her face.

Ravyn felt herself flush under his scrutiny. To deflect its intensity, she thought out loud. "His boots, almost swashbuckling. The dramatic coat. Homespun linen clothes." She smiled. "He's eccentric. Add in the staff – the holly on it might indicate something Druid. But with that long silver hair and beard, well, all you really need is the right hat and you've got the quintessential Merlin-esque wizard." She pursed her lips. "Maybe he's even enchanted the wolves, put them under a spell."

"Not with wild magic. Controlling others? Manipulating things? Those have nothing to do with it." Damien's voice was quiet but firm.

The intensity of his reaction was surprising. Ravyn darted a glance at his face.

He caught her gaze and held it. "The wild, it isn't wild unless it's free."

With his voice as low as it was, Ravyn leaned forward to hear, her eyes still locked with his. A silence followed, broken only by the soft whisper of their breath and a steady drumming of the heart.

The quiet calling of an owl not too far off startled them both, at least enough to break through their little bubble. "What if he wasn't just Merlin-*esque*, this man here?" Damien asked, smoothly picking up the conversation. His attention had dropped back to the tapestry. Where it remained steadfast.

Ravyn swallowed, dragging her focus back to the tapestry as well. "You mean…"

"I think this man, he's Merlin."

His words hung in the air.

Ravyn was silent, as if waiting for him to take them back.

Truth was she was feeling a little queasy what with treading waters such as these, their depths far beyond her original reckoning. Eventually, a small sigh escaping, she began with, "Well." Then stopped before adding, "It would have to be symbolic, obviously. And our search for a wolf-whisperer would be pointless - the wolves would likely be symbols then too."

Voice soft, a smile gently traced its way across Damien's face as he said, "Some stories say Merlin is immortal."

There was silence from Ravyn that stretched for some time as she stared at her companion. Finally, with a caustic look, she retorted with what she'd long been wanting to say, "You can't. Be. Serious."

"Why not?" It was a quick rebuttal. Maybe Damien was looking for a voice of reason to quiet his most wayward suspicions.

Groping for the rational argument that would put the whole kibosh on such a ridiculous idea, Ravyn argued, "For one, there's his tomb. In Merlin's Forest?"

"You yourself suggested it couldn't be his."

"But…" She stopped, frowning. He was right. Switching tack, she pushed back from another angle. "Merlin's just something out of fiction, you know." Clearly her own mental faculties needed sharpening – she should have led with this argument.

Damien shook his head. "Some research, it suggests he's more than an entertaining story. That he's more more like Robin Hood than, I don't know, Captain America or something."

"But Robin Hood wasn't some kind of sorcerer." Her quirked eyebrow said all she needed to about the validity of that point. "It's not like it's outside the realm of reality for someone like him to have existed or something. England's Forest Charter didn't just come out of thin air, you know."

"True." To Ravyn's consternation, he didn't argue against her point, but instead pressed it further. "What if Merlin, he was part of something similar, only earlier?"

Merlin? As a people's hero protecting the forest they belonged to? The thought truly had never occurred to her.

And for good reason.

"Merlin isn't Merlin if he isn't a sorcerer," she scoffed. "And we all know wizards don't exist."

"We do?"

His quiet question hung there in the air between them, Ravyn's blank stare his only answer.

Then, as if she was willing to overlook his momentary lapse of sanity, she had to ask (with a tilt of her chin and only half in jest), "Any chance we might get to Sherwood Forest as part of all this?"

"One day, probably. But I doubt for this assignment."

With a smile at such future possibilities, Ravyn gave in a little, a very tiny little. Folding her arms, she said, "Supposing, just supposing...I'm absolutely not acquiescing to such an absurd idea. But suppose you're right. Merlin existed. He's still alive even. What could that all possibly mean for us?"

"Myth or no, I think Brocéliande is the hint in the tapestry."

"But that's just a legend. There's no such place for real." The holiday had been too busy for much research on the wildwoods of Brittany, but she did find time to look up this.

"Merlin's Forest, if you prefer," he offered. "Up by Paimpont."

Like a deflating balloon, Ravyn gave in. "Because of the schist up there," she said with resignation, remembering their conversation in the Theil.

"Because of the schist up there." Damien smiled.

Thinking on it, she didn't have to accept Damien's outlandish idea that Merlin had actually existed – or even more insane, still did – in order to see the tapestry as a clue. They didn't have to literally find the most legendary wizard in all of Western folklore in order to finish their work assignment, however much it kept trending to the weird and outright bizarre. "Alright, it makes sense...to an extent," she conceded. "If this – thing – " She held up the tapestry between her thumb and forefinger. "Is supposed to give us clues –." Her glance at Damien was highly skeptical. "Then I can see how a Merlin type of figure could be pointing us to Paimpont." She studied the tapestry again before beginning to slowly roll it back up. "Where did you say this came from again?"

Damien was silent for a heartbeat before he answered. "Not all of our assignments come with one of these."

It still wasn't exactly an answer to her question.

"The style seems old," she said. "Like from the time when monks spent lives illuminating books with their illustrations. But it couldn't be…" Her voice trailed off as her eyes sought Damien's.

A shrug was all Damien gave as a reply.

Ravyn prodded, but hesitantly, "If by some weird chance it is, we should be giving it to the proper authorities."

"With things like these," he said quietly. "We are the proper authorities."

Ravyn found herself simply staring at him – again – as she returned the rolled tapestry, placing it in his upturned palm. Swallowing, she found her words once more. "So, um, we do what now? Go to Paimpont and just find wolves?"

Damien nodded, eyes dark pools. "Let's hope it's that easy. The wolves are the key, I'm sure of it." With a sideways look at her, he added, "And Merlin, too. If he's around." His lips pressed into a firm line indicating either determination or, Ravyn fervently hoped, suppressed humor.

Without giving an inch to the preposterous theories Damien posited, Ravyn was intrigued by all she'd read about the Brocéliande forest. Home to fairies (most notably Merlin's rumored soulmate), enchanted pools, ancient megaliths as well as a mecca for Merlin apostolates and a wellspring of lore on the legendary Arthur of the Round Table.

Ravyn hummed as she packed for their journey there. If nothing else, it would definitely make a great setting for one of her romantasy stories someday. To be honest, she was rather surprised at how much she was enjoying her research for this peculiar assignment with both her online and in-person investigations.

The next morning, they swung through Rennes to drop Ravyn's parents at the train station from where they were to embark on what her mother called "a frolic through the countryside" on their own dime before flying home. After buying two tickets, Neeja and Ravyn waited inside for the two men to return with the luggage from the Fiat – packing the little car with the travel retinue of four grown adults earlier that morning had been an adventure in and of itself. The journey from Essé to Rennes was a crammed one.

Just outside the turnstile leading to the boarding platform, Ravyn folded beautifully brocaded cashmere gloves (a Christmas gift from her mother) over the top of her purse, watching with her mom as the train pulled into place. The bright glare of the overhead lights glanced off its shiny metal surface.

"Well." Neeja drew a deep breath as she looked at Ravyn. "Promise you'll be careful, hm?"

"It's just a trial run, Mom. They said it shouldn't be anything dangerous this time."

Carefully scrutinizing her daughter, Neej slowly asked, "Does that imply this position – that is the one you'd commit to, not the trial one – sometimes involves something dangerous?" Her eyebrows threatened to elevate into her hairline.

"Um." Ravyn sucked in her lower lip thinking of Trevor and his role as security, Damien's sweeping for bugs, Bianca's comment about needing a safe place to return to. "I don't entirely know yet," she said cautiously. "But I'll be careful. I promise. If I even decide to hire on permanently."

Lips pursed, Neeja launched into full-on Mom Mode. "I packed a couple extra bags of snack-type food from the cafe in the car for you and Damien," she said. "You have more than that winter dress jacket with you, I assume?"

"Yes, Mom."

"A scarf?"

Ravyn nodded as Neeja went through the usual list down to double-checking Ravyn had all the emergency numbers she'd need, especially being in a foreign country, and that Ravyn's cell phone battery was fully charged.

"You wouldn't think I've been a fully functioning adult for almost two decades," Ravyn complained. But she hugged Neej close as her mom pulled her into a bear-hug.

"Don't forget what I told you about...you know," Neeja whispered as if it wrapped-up everything she'd been saying in the long litany just before – meaning it likely was the one point she'd been angling for all along. At her daughter's blank look, Neeja tilted her head significantly toward the short hallway behind them. Prior to the lengthy spate of last minute motherly advice and concerns over food provisioning, Damien had left down that hall with Samuel to get the older couple's luggage from the Fiat.

Face warming, Ravyn puffed out her cheeks before she said, "Forgetting it is precisely what I'm trying to do, Mother."

Her mom's eyes lit up. "Then it worked. If you want to forget but haven't got past the trying to forget part, then you *are* thinking on it."

Ravyn smiled despite herself. "You're impossible." She affectionately nudged her mom with an elbow. "But I love you for it. And no," she quickly added. "That doesn't mean I'm taking your advice." She tried to look stern. "He's a co-worker, and an attached one at that. Besides there are much more interesting fish swimming in these waters than romance, you know."

"Oh? That's intriguing, coming from my favorite romance writer."

Seeing a way she could squash this nonsense from coming up again, all bravado and speaking the louder as she tried to be clear, Ravyn sallied back with, "Exactly. Remember that's what I do for a living. It's not like I can't imagine a character just as interesting, if not more so, than Damien."

"Right." Eyebrows raised, her mother turned her attention to the pinging phone she held in her hand. "I'll just let you think on that. And think hard, dearie." Checking the incoming text, she smiled. "Your father and Damien have the luggage all squared away." Then her face paled.

Behind them, Damien cleared his throat.

Neeja swiveled to look over her shoulder. "Oh good." Her grin was quick and flashy. "You two are here, eh? Already." She took a deep breath, eyes briefly darting to Ravyn.

Spine rigid, every pixel on her face flushing a deep red, Ravyn didn't dare turn around. Instead she deftly flipped open her purse, finding its innermost contents of much greater interest than anyone (including herself) could have previously imagined.

Her mom stepped in. Briskly brushing at her travel skirt, she slipped an arm through Damien's, turning him toward the vending machines. "Thank-you for making this happen," she told him as they walked away from Ravyn and Samuel. "Christmas without Ravyn wouldn't have been Christmas at all."

Samuel, studying his daughter's face, smiled. "Close call, eh?"

"Totally." She let out her breath. "Dad, do you think he heard?"

"Heard what?"

"Good."

He put an arm around her shoulders. "Your mom's right, you know. But if your new position has you doing what I think you're doing judging by that dolmen we went to, you're right too. There are much more interesting fish swimming in these waters than romance."

"Dad!" Her voice was low but it carried the hysteric lilt of a wail to it. "You mean he did hear?"

"I mean there are much more interesting fish, whatever he may have heard. He's a good one. But it's also good he doesn't know exactly how much you think so too."

Ravyn thought she might find the women's public restroom and camp out there a few weeks. At least until Damien returned to the States.

That not being a viable option, however, their respective goodbyes said, Ravyn didn't think she had ever more regretted seeing her parents off on an adventure, leaving her alone to deal with her own.

Neither she nor Damien said anything to each other.

Except when Ravyn did indeed excuse herself to go to the restroom before hitting the road, prolonging her absence as long as she dared. And Damien muttered something about fetching the car.

C hapter Seventeen

Though the distance to Paimpont wasn't all that far, the hour it took driving westerly to get there felt much longer. Like a sunny day turned unexpectedly gloomy, this was in no small part due to the chill that grew inside the little Fiat between its pair of human occupants. With the interior as tiny as it was, there was little room for distance, yet each quietly made what space they could. Ravyn snugged against her door. Damien's right hand held the wheel as he leaned against the driver's side armrest on his left.

He'd held good to his brief word back at the train station and brought the car around to the pick-up area. There he politely but silently held the passenger door for Ravyn. Purse securely stashed between the seats, as they drove away from the station she'd turned on the radio, filling the void the lack of conversation left behind. Not that she understood a word of what was being sung or said on any station.

They drove through Rennes to the highway. Ravyn pulled out her phone, praying she could pick up internet as they drove. "Might as well research as we drive," she said with more of a whinny than a laugh.

Looking rather sulky – at least to his partner sitting in the seat beside him – Damien glanced at her phone. "About Merlin's Forest?" At her answer in the affirmative, he was gruff in his reply, pulling another cell phone from the center console between the seats. "This phone is the better one to use."

"Why?"

"More secure. It's encrypted."

With a deep breath and only a slightly suppressed sigh, Ravyn complied.

Typing "Merlin's Point" over and over again into the phone, only vaguely aware of the useless results pointing her to housing possibilities in the UK, Ravyn repeatedly assured herself that an apology to Damien would only worsen things. She wasn't entirely sure what he'd heard, but given that her last statement in the conversation with her mom had been the worst, it probably didn't matter if he'd heard anything else they'd said prior to that. But apologizing for that last comment seemed to carry a high likelihood of jumbling things into a worse mess.

Frustrated that the Google results were confined to the UK, Ravyn peered at her search terms, reddened slightly and, hunching her shoulders, braved a glance at Damien as she quickly thumb-tapped more proper terms into the search engine. "Merlin's Forest. Paimpont," she said out loud as if the belated timing of this particular research trajectory had been competently planned all along.

The results she'd been looking for finally rolled in. Finding the site she'd left off with the other day, in a sudden shift Ravyn turned to Damien, extending an olive branch before she could think to stop herself. "That was really nice what you did. Bringing my parents here."

He shrugged but didn't look over at her. "No problem. We were supposed to have you home by Christmas. Family's important."

"Well, thank you for it." Wholly without flirtatious intent she glanced at him from under her lashes, feeling tremendously pleased with herself as she solicitously wrapped it up with the French, "*Merci.*"

That being said, there didn't seem to be anything else to say. Other than to ask how his own holiday went, which, given everything, she was not about to do. So she returned to studying the phone. Things fell silent between them. Damien turned down the radio. The wheels hummed along on the highway pavement.

There were an incredible number of stories regarding Merlin and Arthur, especially

Merlin, in Brittany's Brocéliande. From the legendary sword in the stone to Merlin's demise, the area was rich with folklore about the duo. "I thought Merlin and Arthur were British," she murmured after reading yet another account of Arthur and his Round Table.

"If you talk to folks here, they won't think so, especially about Merlin." Smoothly changing lanes, Damien added, "Arthur, though, he's at that nexus – it connects Albion, the British tribes, the Celts of Brittany, and the Romans, of course."

"Then Albion was real, you think."

"For sure. Albion, remember, it was what Arthur was meant to bring back or, how do you say, revive. Revitalize." The glance he cast her way held a strange look of curiosity. He didn't press it, though, instead wrapping up the mini-history lesson. "Then the Anglo-Saxons invaded the British Isles and complicated everything." He frowned.

But Ravyn was caught on this point. "I thought Britain *was* Anglo-Saxon."

"You and most of the rest of the world." His mouth pressed into a line, expression tired. "That idea, it probably comes from the eugenics movement."

"Meaning," Ravyn guessed, drawing on her own perceptions of what had long rationalized British colonial rule. "The Anglo-Saxon invasion is meant to be an example of so-called inferior tribals being replaced by a so-called superior race?"

With a brief glance her way, Ravyn saw a smile had found its way to his eyes. "You know your history," he said.

"As, clearly, do you." Bookish was the other word Bev had used to describe him. Ravyn supposed they were both proving her right. Yet again. "That time period interests you then?" Ravyn asked, continuing to scroll through her search results.

Just when Ravyn thought he'd left the topic behind he answered, voice soft. "Tribal history is an important key to understanding wild magic." His thumb tapped several beats on the steering wheel. "Especially what's happened to it."

Having already started yet another article in the silence that had followed her question, her reply was more a segue than a direct response. Index finger marking her place, she said, "You have to hear this. Merlin's ghost – " She stopped to look at him directly. "His ghost is believed to be a part of this particular woods. Like he's bound to it physically." Frowning, she corrected her wording, "In an incorporeal way."

"The spirit of nature itself." His eyes flicked momentarily in her direction. "So they say."

"You see I was right, though." She crooked a smile at Damien. "Merlin's not alive." It seemed a ludicrous thing to have to point out. "People pay homage to his ghost there. His *ghost*," she emphasized. Somehow, using the rumored existence of a ghost as a legitimate rebuttal to Damien's claim about Merlin's immortality seemed perfectly rational.

"Unless this ghost is actually Merlin in the flesh and blood."

"Really," she sighed. "How – "

"They say he's the most powerful of the wizards, yeah?"

Lines furrowed her forehead. "Agree to disagree," she murmured in a manner she thought most gracious, forgetting entirely that her original argument was Merlin had never actually existed in the first place. Thumbing through to another page, she suddenly muttered, "Fairy frogs." Ravyn held up the phone for him to see, glanced at the road, thought better of it, and quickly pulled the phone back. "Huge parts of Merlin's Woods are closed this time of year."

"Closed?"

"Yeah." She zoomed in on an image. "There's this military training camp there."

"Military?" Damien glanced in his rearview mirror as if humvees were closing in as they spoke. "And that's what's closed?"

"Well, yeah, it's closed. But that's not all that is." She grimaced. "Most of the woods is either military or private. And almost all the private land closes come fall. For hunting season." Sighing, she added. "It doesn't open again 'til spring."

Damien's thumb tapped a couple steady beats on the steering wheel. *"Ben là."* His voice was low but strained.

She waited for a translation, but none came.

With a flick of the turn signal, he palmed the wheel, making a left onto a smaller road. His thumb-tapping slowed, eyes narrowing.

"You're thinking something."

"Maybe." No elaboration followed.

The road signs were clear enough on the smaller road that even Ravyn understood they marked the way to the village of Paimpont.

Plus the car's GPS indicated their lodging was just ahead.

After driving a good quarter hour from the main road and through a small town, they followed a nearly one-lane road to Le Château du Forêt, a bed and breakfast loitering at the border of the Brocéliande forest. Tall, bare-limbed trees crowded close around a four-story house that appeared steeped in the depths of time. Not quite as far back as Merlin's time, but everything definitely seemed dialed in from a couple centuries back. Thin drifts of snow clung to the panes on long windows which filled every level. The forest, frosted with a white dusting, lay just beyond the willow-bordered lawn.

Unfastening her seatbelt and grabbing her purse, Ravyn looked around for the cashmere gloves her mother had given her, hurriedly checking her purse, jacket pockets, even the glove compartment. "Have you seen my – ?" she began, turning to Damien.

He was already holding out the pair. "These gloves? You dropped them at the train station." His voice was low.

Their eyes met briefly. Both looked away.

Strained eddies from the train station stirred between them. Or so it felt to Ravyn. Slowly pulling on the gloves in question, she wished she could simply gather the courage to apologize head on. But, handwear in place, she merely stared ahead, eyeing the low hedge that accented a stone wall bordering the graveled parking area.

Finally, she hazarded a glance at Damien. As if choking on the words clustered at the back of her throat, she coughed lightly and swallowed hard.

Momentarily fingering the beads on the leather braid wrapped round his wrist a moment, Damien turned to fiddling with his phone, not really looking at it. Ultimately, opening the car door, he shoved the phone in a coat pocket, stopping to take the keys out of the ignition as the car pinged alarm at him for leaving them behind.

Pushing out of the car, Ravyn gave another delicate cough. "So, what's the plan?" she ventured, hoping to sidestep the other problem completely.

"Plan?"

"Yeah. Do you want to just move on with things? Or should we do something else?"

Damien studied her over the roof of the car. "Move on? " His expression was vague. "You mean…" His eyes, guarded, watched her as if ferreting out her next move.

"Brocéliande. Of course."

His chin jerked up, and he nodded slowly. "The forest is really closed right now?"

"Ninety percent of it," Ravyn agreed. Her bright manner, intended to lighten the tension, was totally inappropriate to the snafu the closure caused them. "But we can still look around the public land. Looks like there are a lot of paths and marked monuments we can legally access, even on some of the private land. And the woods right around the chateau are open."

Damien shook his head. "It's the wildest places we need to find. And those won't be on the trails."

That's kind of what Ravyn had thought.

"We'll need some maps," he said. "Of the whole forest."

"You're not thinking of going on to private lands anyway?" Ravyn narrowed her eyes. "They may patrol the area. Like they do at the Hidden Mountains.

"Which is why I won't be asking you to do this."

"I have a story to write," she said quietly, pulling her backpack from the car.

"And now you'll have the time to get started." He grabbed his duffle out of the trunk, shutting the hatchback loudly.

"Meaning," she continued firmly, ignoring his suggestion. "I'm coming with you."

Shaking his head, Damien started walking to the inn.

Ravyn shouldered her backpack, the weight of the things she should say still heavy. She may not be able to apologize for what was said at the station, but there were other things she could share. "Damien," she rather reluctantly called after him as she started to catch up. "There's something you should know."

He slowed, turning to look back at her. Duffle bag over his shoulder, he squinted at the sunlight reflecting off the snow.

"I saw – that guy. The one that was with Elinor?"

He set the duffle on the ground at his feet, frowning. "Here?"

"No," she hastened to assure him. "Before Christmas. At the market in Essé. I thought you'd want to know…" She hesitated, doubting the wisdom of diving into this affair of the heart when it wasn't her business. "I just thought you'd be happy to know that they've left France by now. At any rate, he *said* they were leaving right after Christmas."

Damien hesitated, nodded, then picked up his bag. "Yes," he said as he walked again toward the inn. "I know."

"I guess the guy's her – " Ravyn stopped to stare at his retreating back. "Wait – you know?" she began and hurried to catch up with him.

Inside Le Château du Fôret, hefty burgundy brocade curtains hung from the floor to the ceiling matching the heavy rugs laid over marble floors. Encountering such somber yet magnificent opulence, Ravyn hesitated in the doorway – and not only because she waited on Damien to answer her query.

Which he didn't. Of course.

He held the door for her. As she walked through, he surveyed the woods and fields beyond as if searching for something.

"Damien?"

"Let's get checked in," he said brusquely, still not quite looking at her.

Evidently she wasn't the only one with important things left unsaid from over the last few days.

As Damien talked with the desk clerk, Ravyn eyed the stalwart cherry-brown banisters. A bas relief garland was carved on them, loops of it tracing the stairway as it made its way to a landing then split in two, each staircase heading to the upper floors. Although Ravyn felt a portrait of Dorian Gray or even Dracula seemed more fitting, a massive yet stunning painting of a woman in a beautiful scarlet dress took up nearly all of the vertical wall space on the landing. Lovely as she was, the painted woman's eyes seemed to follow her as Ravyn slowly paced beside Damien, waiting. Though the clerk seemed friendly, Ravyn certainly would not mind if their stay at the chateau was far from a lingering one.

Unlike their rooms – with décor steeped in dark velvet curtains, thick ceiling beams, and squat, solid four-poster beds – Damien's mood was cheery when they met for supper. Though Ravyn hadn't forgotten that he still had to answer her question – her latest unanswered one at any rate – she let the matter be. Except for a quick foray into Paimpont for dinner and to pick up maps of the area, the two of them set up camp in Damien's room. As Damien pored over Google Earth and all the other map material he could get his hands on, Ravyn thoroughly combed the internet, locating the wildest places of significance to their work, especially as related to the tapestry.

Brocéliande was a complex place, much more so than La Roche aux Fées. The maps were densely packed with megaliths and sites marking the legends of Arthur and Merlin. A steady stream of questions came from Damien about these as he sleuthed out the best routes to the wildest places.

With the area rich in history (at least of the folkloric kind), if Ravyn's father had been there his experience in all things historical may have made the information easier to sort through. Then again he may simply have settled in for a long winter's research and led them into many more rabbit holes than they already managed to stumble into on their own. Such as when Ravyn, curious if Le Lac de Viviane was in a wild place (it wasn't) got caught in a thirty-minute tumble down a research hole about exactly who the Fairy Viviane was – Merlin's true love or a deceitful fairy collecting the wizard as one of her many conquests. This last was more due to Tennyson's poem. Viviane it turned out, like Morgana, suffered greatly in her reputation as the centuries drew closer to the modern era. It was all totally irrelevant to their current quest but utterly fascinating nonetheless.

Hours of screentime later, Ravyn pushed away from the desk for one of her regular stretch breaks. "Maybe coming back in the spring after the hunting season wouldn't be such a bad idea. Give us more time to get some solid research on the place." She rubbed sore eyes with her index fingers. "If MegaLit would pay for another trip to France."

"For sure. Travel and research is a big part of what we do." The golden glow of a circadian adjusted screen reflected across Damien's face in the dimly lit room.

"I could get used to that," she murmured, attention returning to her screen.

With a sharp glance at her, he leaned back in his chair, hesitated, then asked, "*Vraiment?*"

Ravyn absently raised an eyebrow as she scrolled through a blog on a history of Albion. It wasn't clear if what Damien had just said required a response or not.

Damien's lips parted, but he was silent. Then he went ahead and spoke anyway. "Then you're thinking of accepting the position?"

No doubt the time to make that decision would approach sooner than she was prepared for. "Um, maybe," she said. "There's a lot to recommend it." She didn't look at him directly.

Damien stretched long legs in front of him, pushing his laptop aside. "If there's anything that can help, let me know as you think it through, okay?"

It was devastatingly embarrassing to note that far too many questions bouncing around at the back of her head were, apparently, more of a reflection of her career as a romance writer than anything that directly pertained to the position at hand. Not one of these passed her lips. Indeed, she kept her mouth pressed tightly closed to ensure they did not and simply shook her head instead.

"Elinor," he offered so quietly Ravyn almost missed it. "She's someone you might want to know more about?"

"Elinor?" She stuttered over the name. "I don't – no. I don't need to know about your relationships." Her cheeks felt as if they were blazing, particularly given the line of questioning that had been silently firing away in her head just moments before.

There was silence for a few heartbeats. Then Damien asked, slowly coming to lean forward, elbows resting on the table, "Our relationship, how did you know about it?"

From the way he said it, it was difficult to tell whether the romance with Elinor was past or present. "I'd have to be blind not to see it," she said even as she felt let down somehow.

"I suppose," he muttered, looking at his hands.

"You saw her over Christmas?" Her blood pulsed a little faster at the temerity she felt in asking this. "I mean, after the Solstice?"

With a slight hesitation, Damien said, "I didn't come back before Elinor left the country. I made sure of it."

It wasn't a straightforward answer. "Alright," Ravyn said having suspected something of the sort though she remained unreasonably curious about the details. As she returned to scrolling, she noted Damien was still watching her.

It was some minutes until he prodded, "You don't ask why."

"It's your business," she said, shrugging, proud of her polite but professionally distanced tone.

"If you join us, this thing with Elinor," he said quietly. "It'll be your business too."

Ravyn looked at him over the screen of her laptop, not entirely certain how to respond to that. Surely even vengeful girlfriends, or ex-girlfriends, drew a line at messing with a person's coworkers. "Why?" she ventured eventually.

"All Bianca will let me say now is that she's more than mere competition."

Even her new boss thought Ravyn was a sucker for falling at Damien's feet immediately? This was getting a little much.

Perhaps something about her thoughts flickered across her face as Damien was quick to add, "I mean, Elinor, she's not one of our magazine competitors. But the people she works for, they're very skillful at trying to stop what we do for MegaLit."

Ravyn studied him. "She's trying to stop us from publishing?"

Lips pressed in a thin line, Damien hesitated yet again before agreeing. "More or less."

"And you're involved with her."

"Was," he said swiftly, eyes trained on his steepling fingers. "Was involved with her." He didn't add more.

Ravyn waited but when nothing further was forthcoming and Damien still didn't look up, she simply said, "Okay then." It wasn't entirely clear how this information might affect her decision. Slowly closing the lid to her laptop, she took a deep breath. "It's a beautiful night." Her breathing grew shallow though at such a brashly uncharacteristic move on her part. "We could take a walk."

He studied her, nodding but with eyes narrowing almost imperceptibly.

For a moment Ravyn thought he was going to bring up the whole embarrassing situation back at the train station, but, after a few moments, he said, gently, "It's late, eh? Maybe we should leave it for another time."

"Of course." She stood abruptly, thankful for the dim light as she felt the heat rise again in her cheeks. "I didn't mean to keep you." Quickly gathering her papers, hard drive, and pen, she stuffed them into her computer case.

Walking Ravyn to the door, Damien held it open. Reaching out before she left, he placed a hand on her forearm. "I'm glad," he said quietly, looking down at her. "Glad this position is something you're thinking of accepting. You should know, MegaLit is behind you one hundred percent." He pressed his palm gently against her arm. "*I'm* behind you one-hundred percent." Then he let go.

"Behind me?" she echoed.

He raised his eyebrows slightly, smiling in assent.

"Thanks," Ravyn said even as her forehead puckered with curiosity. As she made her way into the hall, Damien's door shut behind her with a soft click. On impulse, Ravyn stopped by her room only to grab a winter coat then silently slipped outside for a starlit walk of her own.

Though nothing untoward happened that night, in retrospect had Ravyn fully understood what Damien had just tried to tell her, she likely would have forsaken the joys of a solitary stroll in a foreign land no matter how starry the skies or how softly refreshing the winter breeze sighing from the fabled woods nearby.

Still when wild magic calls, it calls. And it, too, has a way of protecting its own.

Chapter Eighteen

Despite her earlier stated objections to plunging into the wilds of forbidden territory, the next morning Ravyn nevertheless had a tune to hum as she prepped her hiking pack and nibbled toast and yogurt down in the inn's surprisingly beautiful and airy breakfast nook. Indeed almost everything about the place was lighter and brighter than it had seemed on their arrival. Perhaps it was the streaming sunlight of the French morning coming in through the long and plentiful windows. Or maybe the anticipatory delight of a deep forest stroll into the famed home of Merlin, Wild Wizard of the Woods.

It was all of these. But more too.

Last night in her walk through the meadows surrounding the inn, the blackly silhouetted forms of the forest had circled a starry, moonless sky while the Milky Way arched overhead. A pair of owls held a softly owlish conversation in the dark as brisk nighttime breezes stirred. If ever she could believe magic truly was afoot in the worldly realm, it was at such a time.

In her dream that night she walked a path of stars, sprinkled there as if growing like wildflowers beneath her feet. A dark gray wolf walked with her. Never near, but never too far away. She woke to the echoes of his voice. "You are so loved," it said.

And that all cast a radiant bit of rightness to the morning.

The feeling didn't dissipate even as at the appointed nine o'clock hour – her backpack slung over a shoulder, winter coat already on – she knocked on Damien's door. And he didn't answer.

"Grumble," Ravyn said for lack of a more descriptive word and made her way down to the desk as a suspicion slowly dawned.

Not having picked up much French over the last week or so, Ravyn took out her phone, pulling up her translator app. *"Avez-vous des messages à me faire?"* she asked the clerk with an uncertain smile. She must not have messed up the pronunciation too badly (and likewise the app with the translation) for he replied, *"Oui. Un moment, s'il vous plaît"* which she vaguely understood did actually mean she may indeed have a message waiting for her.

It was no surprise then when the clerk returned, handing her one of the hotel-supplied envelopes. Opening it with her index finger, Ravyn pulled out the small sheets inside.

Damien was sparse in conveying his message. It consisted of a map and a quickly scrawled note that read, "Back by three. Maybe have your bags packed." It was signed, *"À tantôt"* which meaning Ravyn could only guess at. Or look up on the translator...which proved to be of no help.

The map itself was slightly more informative, depicting the entirety of the Paimpont Forest. Damien had starred a couple sites including Le Fontaine de Barenton and Le Chêne des Hindrés. Googling these things, she found that the first was a fountain of some sort down a trail evidently remote enough it wasn't easily accessible to all. The second was an old oak tree that could be accessed almost all year round, including today. On the map at least, both looked to be fairly isolated spots in terms of human development. Meaning they presented possibilities for what she and Damien were looking for.

If only he had waited for her.

As to the other part of his message, she could only assume he meant she should be ready to leave when he returned.

Feet not so sprightly on the staircase as they had been earlier, she did as bid only to return about a half hour later nearly springing down the stairway. Damien may be off exploring on his own, but she had legs too. As an American illiterate in French, how much trouble with the law could she get into if she wandered into any restricted woods around here? Surely they'd understand the language barrier.

"It's frigid out," the clerk called to her as she passed by the desk. So he knew English. That'd make it easier next time. Ravyn glanced at the thermometer. Five degrees. For an alarmed moment Ravyn worried about Damien and frostbite before remembering to compensate for Celsius. Lower forties in Fahrenheit. Not exactly frigid where she came from, but she simply smiled anyway. "*Merci*," she replied as she pushed out the door, happy to feel a growing comfort level with the language. That one word anyway.

Leaving the inn, parking lot, and especially the road behind, she strode across a meadow to the part of the Brocéliande forest that encircled its grassy borders, barely glancing at what could have been a "No Trespassing" sign at the edge of the wood.

The air was cool and crisp. Shadows from the trees stretched long with the winter's morning sun. Still yesterday's light snow had melted in all but the shadiest nooks. Even there brown ferns held dewdrops near the tips of their fronds though the moss beneath was white with frost. In a scattering of smaller trees, eddies of mist rose like so much whimsy as sunshine found other hidden alcoves of dew and rime.

Sorting legend from fact was usually a complicated business. But in these woods it didn't even seem necessary. Worlds blended here. Graceful moss-laden roots gripped the earth like sinewy fingers. Birch leaned lithely over woodland pools, preening at their own reflections. And what were her own legs but mere uprooted trunks roaming freely across the landscape?

Even the crow cawing on her approach as he lifted from the limb of a grand old oak, its buds already swelling for spring, seemed the eyes of the forest. He caught a thermal, spiraling into the blue and the puffy clouds at altitudes higher than most crows dared. Coasting for minutes on end, he suddenly pulled his wings close to flip left and down then right, stretching into a full glide, skimming the treetops.

The crow's sudden screech seemed to bring all to a halt.

Ravyn looked around, silent as the woods about her.

The crow too was quiet as he flapped quickly, wings near-silent, to other regions of the forest.

Though she couldn't be sure, there seemed to be the dull whir of a soft motor reverberating through the trees. But she saw nothing.

Uneasy, Ravyn cut another small arrow on the bark of a beech marking her passage. Never keen on being the witting (or unwitting) fool when she could help it, Ravyn had marked the trees this way methodically ever since she'd entered the Brocéliande. The scare she'd had in the Hidden Mountains had almost immediately led to starting a self-directed crash course in natural navigation, though she'd only just begun to make her way through a stack of Tristan Gooley books on the subject. Still she knew enough now to know the passage of the sun as it related to the compass rose and to read a tree for branch growth and the hints that it carried about the southerly directions. Navigating by spider webs and growth rings on stumps waited in the chapters ahead, although Ravyn wasn't exactly planning on asking every arachnid she ran across to point her the way home.

Not wanting to take any chances, however, she'd marked a small notch of an arrow in this beech and that as she passed, pointing the way back.

At one such beech growing close to a gathering of spruce, a sleepy patch of isolated snow nestled beneath conifer boughs. The beauty of the little scene drew her attention to the signs of passage from a rather large animal. At first she mistook the prints for just another ambling domesticate like herself.

Until she considered it again.

The partial imprint of a large paw, easily as big as her palm if the track had been whole, had melted the snow just enough to make it translucent. Ravyn was no expert tracker but she knew it was significant the claw marks showed. Given that she'd left the human neighborhood behind an hour or so ago, on mindful reconsideration it didn't seem at all likely it came from a denizen of the dominantly human world.

Grabbing a pen and a piece of paper, one on which Damien had written his message, she did her best to accurately draw out the size of the track. As added evidence, she snapped a photo with her phone.

Eager to get to a place with cell signal so she could visit a tracking app, Ravyn picked up her pace, shifting from a saunter into a hike, pausing only long enough to carefully fold the paper and slip it into her pack.

Walking swiftly, feet slipping on frosty logs and damp leaves, she almost didn't hear the whirring as it neared overhead.

A sudden croak from a raven winging by made her look up. As she did so, a dim dark form the size of a large bird but clunky in shape was visible through the limbs of nearby trees. Ducking quickly behind the girth of a giant oak, she instinctively burrowed into the cold, wet leaves at the base of the trunk there.

The drone thrummed by on the far side of the tree.

Nestling against the tree, fingers wiggling into loamy soil, she waited until even the softest whisper from the machine was gone. Noting the direction of its passage, she found she was able to safely continue her original path. Ravyn set off more rapidly than before, following her notches back.

Arriving only a little after one, she was surprised to see Damien in the parking lot, loading his duffle bag and laptop case into the trunk of the car. Ravyn stopped short, half wondering if he was somehow preparing to leave her there. Just then he looked up, saw her standing on the edge of the meadow and gave a little wave. Jogging to meet her halfway, first thing he said was "Your bags, are they packed?"

"Do they need to be?" she countered, still sore he'd left her behind.

"It would be best," he said.

"You got caught."

He shook his head, shoving hands into his coat pockets. "But it's likely I was seen."

With a rueful look, she grimaced. "I had a close encounter myself."

Mouth quirking into a half smile, Damien reached over, pulling a brown oak leaf from her hair. "This, does it have something to do with that?"

"Probably."

But his smile faded quickly. "We should leave."

Ravyn nodded, handing him her pack. "I'll get the rest," she said and hurried to the inn.

Chapter Nineteen

Nestled cozily as she so often was in her warm and homey garret, Ravyn had never truly been part of a clandestine operation before, outside of her fiction that is. Though wholly lacking any intention of being in such a situation again, she did have to admit to the sheer invigorating thrill of it all.

"A security car or two may have followed me a stretch." Damien grimaced as gravel spurted from under the tires when he pulled out of the inn's parking area. Though he kept the speed appropriate to the small backroad, Ravyn could see the tension in the white of his knuckles where he gripped the steering wheel.

"For trespassing? Surely that must happen all the time."

"Probably. But if someone's put them on alert for something more dangerous, it would mean every little infraction counts."

"You mean like – " Ravyn eyed him, concern mounting over what exactly he was hinting about himself. With his mysterious ways, her imagination encountered little to check it.

"Try the terror alerts," he said. "They're posted on the US Embassy page."

"Terrorism?" Her voice squeaked as she pulled out her phone, shrinking a little inside herself as she quickly checked the US State Department – and nearly choked. Her voice was tight when she said, "They've issued a Level Two Advisory." The pulse in her throat fluttered. "It's because they think terrorists are planning attacks." She looked at Damien. "This…" Gathering her courage, she pressed, "You're saying this…this is you?"

At the intersection with the main road, a police-like vehicle slowed to turn down the road they were on. Damien lowered his face with Ravyn outright scrunching down in the passenger seat.

"What's the date of the advisory?" He was calm, turning the opposite direction from where they'd come in yesterday. In the rearview mirror, Ravyn could see him keeping an eye on the patrol car that had passed them.

Struggling to see her phone, pinned as she was between the seat and the glove compartment thanks to her emergency-activated downward slump – a pose she remained reluctant to relinquish – Ravyn swiped through the numerous apps she'd unintentionally provoked with her swift and sudden maneuverings and found the terror alert she'd pulled up only minutes earlier.

Damien was right. It had been issued in May.

"France is at Level Two a lot," Damien explained. "But we can take the backroads to

Paris anyway. Less patrols, eh?" Evidently seeing she still needed some reassurance, he added, "Don't worry. We've been reported as toughs on other assignments but still made a good escape."

"Sooo," she said slowly, carefully. "You're saying you're not a terrorist?"

Briefly taking his eyes from the road, he gave her a puzzled look. "Terrorist?"

Ravyn gave a curt nod, eyes steady on his face.

A smile flickered there. "You mean like pipe-bombs, violence, setting fire to Teslas? That kind of thing? Absolutely, no."

Her immediate fear of riding in a car with a terrorist dissipated.

But he wasn't finished. "By other definitions?" He looked at her again, a quirk to his smile. "If you mean things like releasing the crickets from our high school dissection lab, then yeah. But that definitely wasn't in France."

She looked at him sideways, not exactly sure if he was kidding her or not. Besides, she was okay with cricket liberation. More than okay. With another secretive look his way, Ravyn emerged from her partial hidey-hole in the passenger-side footwell. Pushing herself back into a normal seating position, she caught Damien glancing in the rearview mirror for a second time. "What is it?" she whispered as if there were others tuning in. He didn't have to tell her as he stepped on the accelerator. "Cop's following us, isn't it?" she prodded.

He didn't answer.

"For trespassing? This is silly." Ravyn sat bolt upright, head swiveling to look back. Sure enough, what looked to be the same patrol car as earlier (though, really, it's not like a person could tell them apart) was now a ways behind. "I mean, it is just for trespassing, right?"

"It's the only illegal thing I've done. What else someone may have called in, that I don't know." He took the first left in a fairly swift fashion at a sort of triangular roundabout.

Ravyn gripped the dash with one hand, surrendering her questions to the pressing turmoil of the moment.

Eyes trained on the twisting road, he said, "Bianca should know what's going on. The phone's between the seats."

"You want me to call? Right now?" Her tone was incredulous.

"The center console, it has the encrypted phone, yeah? You can put it on speaker."

Not entirely certain about her partner's current state of sanity, Ravyn nevertheless found his phone and followed through. A woman's authoritative voice filled the small car. "You two on your way home?" It was Bianca.

When the answer came back in a vague sort of way, her sigh was audible. "What did you do this time, Damien?" she asked.

Raising her eyebrows, Ravyn looked at her partner. "This time?" she whispered.

With a slight smile, Damien shrugged. "Trespassing, Bianca, nothing more. It's just the way the thing turned out."

A rolling forest of bare trees, snow sparse underneath them, whipped by on both sides of the narrow road.

"You got caught."

"Not yet." Damien slowed for a sharp curve. "But things aren't looking so great right now."

"You need an Extrication?"

That sounded dire. Ravyn's eyebrows rose again.

"Probably." Damien was cool in his reply as if this sort of thing happened every day.

Ravyn swallowed.

"I'll get Stacy working on it." There was a tapping in the background as if Bianca were drumming her long fingernails on that glass-top desk of hers. "You have your alternate ids on you?"

"Yep." His tone was curt.

"You may need them." Bianca's fingernails continued tapping her desk. "Ravyn, text me your GPS numbers, would you? We'll be in touch. Call if you need us sooner."

Damien accelerated into a hairpin curve.

Alarmed, Ravyn glanced behind. Police lights whirled. But they weren't near. Her stomach flipped. So this was really happening.

The Fiat's tires squealed. Damien took another tight curve too fast. Ravyn grabbed the dash with both hands.

"We can't just outrun them," she said. "Why not pull over? It's only a dumb misunderstanding."

"With all this, it's probably more than that." He accelerated into another curve. "Not by my doing," he added quickly.

It wasn't like he could divulge his entire life story right then. Ravyn gave a short nod. "Okay." For now.

Suddenly, Damien let off the accelerator, pumped the brakes, eyes on a gated drive just ahead.

"We can't just smash into that!" Ravyn's right foot pressed hard against the floor. She gripped the seat tightly.

He acknowledged that fact. But kept going. And worse. To her consternation, their speed was increasing.

"Um, Damien?" Her words were shrill. She pointed to a sign clearly announcing "Danger." In English. It stood at the end of the drive.

He nodded. Even as he accelerated yet again. The tires hit the shoulder. Snow and dirt spewed by the windows.

Ravyn's voice pealed into a wordless squeal. One hand clutched the armrest. The other the edge of the seat.

The Fiat slowed suddenly. There was a small space between the woods and gatepost. The car squeezed through, breaking tree limbs. One screeched along the side of the vehicle side.

Pushing through the narrow passage, a two track, barely traveled, stretched beyond into a pine plantation.

Damien pushed the acceleration. Fast. The electric engine hummed low. The drive was rough.

In seconds, the gate was a distant landmark.

Damien slowed then stopped. The rearview mirror reflected his backward glance.

Ravyn swung around to watch out the back window.

The police car rushed by on the road, lights blazing.

"Think we're safe?" Face flushed, the pulse in Ravyn's neck throbbed as it had rarely done before.

"We'll see. Those coordinates, yeah? They've been texted?"

She'd forgotten. Primarily because she wasn't precisely sure how to look those up for their exact location.

Damien picked up the phone, punching buttons. "There," he said. "Done."

"So now what?" Prepping to flee into the woods, Ravyn ogled the pines for a good escape route with lots of cover.

"We wait."

"Wait?" The adrenaline that shook her body even now wanted her to flee.

But they sat quietly. Ravyn huffed in little breaths, but surreptitiously, pretending the excitement hadn't made her feel as if she'd just run a marathon. If she got so out of breath just sitting in a car being chased, what would happen if she ever had to actually run in order to escape? Finally she caught her breath enough to ask, "Where'd you learn to drive like that?" Tension roughened her voice.

"Practice" was all he said.

Silence filled the car again.

Wanting to prod Damien about the nature of this practice he'd had, Ravyn instead settled for something with a little more immediate relevance. Besides with words like Extricator and Extrication being bandied about, it seemed prudent to learn a bit more about what lay ahead. "Um, what is it exactly we're waiting for?"

Damien turned to her, mouth quirking into a partial smile. "Sorry. It's easy to forget you're not used to this."

At least she wasn't exuding a "newbie" attitude.

"Stacy'll have someone here soon," he added.

"Have someone?"

"An Extricator."

That sounded alarming.

"Whoever comes to get us, they'll take us to a private airfield. We'll probably borrow someone's jet. Then we'll fly out of the country with little security interference."

Tidy plan.

"With any luck, Stacy will have it so that we disappear off the grid."

"All this, just for taking an illegal walk on some land this morning." It seemed pretty incredible to Ravyn.

Tugging at the braided leather around his wrist, he said, "I suspect someone probably hacked the police system. Messed with the records. Like I said, it's happened before." Seeing her face, he gave her a small smile. "All this will make more sense if you decide to go deeper in with us."

He watched her face as if looking for some hint of her thoughts, probably curious how it all affected her opinion about the trial position, one she was – at the moment – eager to terminate. Then again, he could just be wondering whether he felt more like tacos or hamburger for dinner tonight.

In reply, Ravyn only nodded – as if she knew what he was talking about – and looked into the pines. "You saw the 'Danger' sign back there, right?" The calm manner in which she asked this surprised even herself.

Damien dipped his head. "Yep. Big game hunting."

"Big game hunting?" Peering into the dense growth of trees for large and fleeing creatures, she asked, "Like wisent?" She'd read only yesterday they'd been common in this area long ago.

His chuckle was a soft one. "More like smaller animals. The deer, for example. Though some Red Stags can weigh a lot. Six hundred pounds." Breaking the silence that followed, he added, his tone more serious, "Or the wild boar. Keep a good watch because – and maybe you know this – it's rutting season."

Ravyn's spine seemed to tidy itself into a stiffly upright position on its own accord. So much for taking a little amble while they waited for the Extricator. She still wasn't precisely sure who – or what – that was.

Suddenly Damien himself straightened, eyes on the sideview mirror. "They just went by again, the police, retracing their route."

"Then they know they lost us."

"Probably yes." Forehead creasing, he picked up his phone, looked at the screen, then moved to put it back when it rang in his hand.

"The Extricator's there." It was Stacy. "But he can't fit, he said. Something about a gate? He's waiting at the road. Bring the car. He'll get it returned."

"Okay." Damien gave the phone to Ravyn, speaker still on. "Ready?" he asked, looking at her.

She nodded. From the phone, Ravyn heard Bianca's fingernails tap dance in the background.

Expertly turning the car around in that tight space, Damien accelerated down the two-track. The gate grew larger. Something big and silver-shiny lurked behind it. To Ravyn it looked sort of like a gleaming shoebox.

Damien slowed. "*Non*, *non*, no way," he muttered. "Stacy? You can't be serious."

"What?" she replied. "Hey, I know a guy. "

There was silence.

"And you totally don't have to worry about the whole not road legal thing," Stacy added.

Ravyn looked at Damien.

His expression was unreadable.

"Not road legal?" Ravyn asked, tentative.

"Yeah." At Ravyn's interjection, Stacy's tone had hardened a little. "He's a visitor there, so he's got a permit."

Sounds of a sort of tussle came over the phone then Trevor came on. "Not legal? What'd Stace do now, Damien?"

"Just ask her."

A muffled conversation broke in waves from the other side of the speakerphone, interrupted by an explosive exclamation or two. Then it was quiet. Even Bianca was silent.

Ravyn exchanged glances with Damien.

Moments later, Trevor came back on. "Geez, Damien. I'm sorry. Looks to be the only thing. But, Stace, could you have found something a bit more conspicuous?"

"Hide in plain sight," Stacy said, her voice soft as it came through like dulled background noise. "And anyway, it's not like we have a lot of contacts as nearby as he is.

"I'd suggest getting in the truck asap, cyber or no." It was Bianca's voice. Hers came through crisp and clear. "It won't be a long drive. And the police records show the local force knows the truck, so it shouldn't attract the worst kind of attention."

Damien sighed, eyebrows raised at Ravyn. Clearly such a thing was not on his bucket list. "Just this, don't bring it up everyday," he muttered.

Chapter Twenty

Despite its exterior, the doors to the odd (what some might call futuristic) vehicle opened more or less like any other from the outside. At least once she and Damien figured out there was a button to push instead of a handle to pull. Ravyn had expected some sort of door design that mimicked a Klingon ship-wing or *Back to the Future*'s DeLorean. The interior didn't disappoint, however. At least if a person liked the sterile spaceship ambience kind of thing. Which she didn't exactly, but still it was more in line with what she'd expect to find.

"*Wesh*," a man in shades said from the driver's seat.

This was a new sort of salutation for Ravyn, and as Damien greeted him in kind, she simply smiled a little, hoping to show she didn't mean to be unfriendly with her complete lack of conversational French.

But the driver's English marked him as American, though that was something Ravyn hardly noticed, working as she did to figure out what he meant by his next statement, "Luggage can go in the frunk." To her surprise, Damien put their bags where the engine would be on any normal automobile. But Ravyn coolly dumped her backpack in with the rest as though she hadn't ever a doubt in the world that this was how it worked.

The vehicle was fast, near silent, and certain to outrun any members of the law who might be tempted to dare a chase after it. It easily got them to their mystery destination. Not a cop car in sight.

A small jet waited in the private airfield, woods edging the borders. Caught up in the excitement of the last little while, Ravyn had nearly forgotten how she felt about the prospect of flying. Nearly. But that prospect now loomed indubitably large and certain on the heavily-treed horizon, a horizon that had little room for take-off. Or so it seemed to her.

Eyeballing the jet where it sat sleek and waiting, her stomach clenching, Ravyn hesitated to open the door before realizing she didn't know how anyway.

"Our chariot, I believe." Damien too studied the plane a moment before pressing a button on the door's arm rest. It swung open.

Simple enough. At least the getting out the door part. Ravyn took a deep breath and followed suit.

Luggage out of the frunk, their driver didn't linger over goodbyes. " 'Later," he said, with a one finger wave and drove off so silently it was more of a glide away.

Expecting the low-key elegance of another MegaLit jet, the waiting jet was anything but. Inside a pastel pink shag carpet lay thickly throughout the cabin. Seats were covered in a fluffy white material. Silver stars studded the ceiling. Mirrors gilded with silver frames dotted the walls.

Pausing behind Ravyn in the doorway, Damien let out a low whistle. "Wonder who Stacy called for this."

Drawn to the luxurious seating, Ravyn dropped her luggage on the floor and sat down. The fluffy seats seemed inclined to devour her whole. Pushing herself out of the comfiness almost immediately, she tended to her bags. There would be time enough to puddle her muscles while crossing the Big Pond.

Damien grabbed her large duffle bag, squaring it away in a nearby compartment. "Bianca had a jet like this once," he said.

"Bianca?"

"Hard to believe, eh? But she did. Her first one."

"Lives of the rich, huh?"

Damien shrugged, then picked up his own backpack and found another empty compartment. He was so silent that he startled her with a follow-up as she was unpacking her laptop, water bottle and other getting-comfy essentials. Long silences were clearly a habit of his, but she had yet to get used to it. "She wasn't always," he said.

Ravyn frowned, trying to recall what they'd been talking about.

"Bianca," he explained, accurately interpreting the confusion writ across her face. "She didn't always have money. The complete opposite actually."

That was news. "You knew her before?"

Damien nodded. In the conversational silence that followed, he slipped out of his winter jacket and hung it over one of the chairs. Ravyn's curiosity kept her quiet as she waited for additional info. Finally he expanded on that point. "We shared a certain sort of...work...in common."

The way he said *that* made things sound even more mysteriously intriguing than before. "Really? What sort of work?" she prompted

"Just, uh, just work."

Which, as he evidently intended, did little to explain things.

As Damien didn't offer more, Ravyn prodded again, perching on the edge of her chair, "So when she got this money – "

"Won," Damien interrupted. "She won it."

After a long, rather startled look, Ravyn added, "Okay. Won it." She looked at him again but continued when he didn't expand on that idea. "One of her first thoughts was to look for a plane full of luxurious fluff?"

A little smile lit his face as he glanced at her. "Let's just say that Bianca, she was young. Things took a while to get situated, to come into focus for her." Settling into the seat next to hers, he turned on his phone, thumb-scrolling down the screen.

Escalade? Private jet? A Northwoods Barbie-doll mansion? These were things coming into focus? But Ravyn said nothing, only slumping into the comfy chair with a sigh – not a little from exasperation at the perpetually impermeable air of mystery eternally hovering about. Exhaustion won out over her curiosity, though, and she fully succumbed to the lure of the fluffy white seats, looking lazily around as she did so for signs of a well-stocked snack bar. It was long past time for a little bit of chocolate – at least if it was within easy reach.

Then the plane started to move, and she lost every bit of appetite, hands reaching to clench the furrily covered armrests. Until she remembered her seatbelt, that is. With a quick grasp and click of the belt, she straightened in her furry, fluffy chair for a white-knuckled take-off.

Somewhere over the mid-Atlantic they got a call. Turned out their afternoon escape attempt had been in vain.

But not in the way that might sound.

Ravyn had begun to show Damien her images of the large paw tracks, taken from what seemed a lifetime ago. "Bear? Wolf? Big dog?" she asked. "I haven't had a chance to upload these to a tracking app yet and check them out."

"Good thing," Damien said, leaning closely over her sketch, arm warm against hers, as he explained. "To protect the wolf, it's better to use screenshots. Those don't have any GPS coordinates in the metadata."

The complexly technical point was lost to the more interesting latter. "You really think these are from a wolf?"

"From the size in your drawing, the details in the photo? Oh, yeah."

Pupils dilated, Ravyn lowered her voice. "Should we go back?"

"Well – " His phone rang. Looking at the caller id, he frowned but answered. "Bianca?"

It was Stacy, as it turned out, calling at Bianca's behest. "The cops weren't after you at all," she said without preamble, emphasizing the final two words in that sentence. Her voice was flat, matter-of-fact. The cracking sound had to be either a bad signal or Stacy with her gum. "Just some dumb local who drives a Fiat and keeps breaking the speed limit. At least that's what the police report said. Took forever to find *that* online." This last was a muttered aside.

There was silence on the plane after Stacy's bit of intel.

Having lowered her eyes at the news that all the zoom-zoom-zoom and squealing of tires that had marked their exit from Paimpont was completely unnecessary, Ravyn couldn't help but glance at Damien through her lashes.

His cheeks were tinged a slight shade of near-pink, almost matching the jet's shag carpet. "Guess that's good, eh?" he said, jawline taut.

"I guess." Stacy snapped her gum.

Ravyn dropped her gaze. All authorial hopes of having a plotline full of shadowy international intrigue for her story on La Roche dissipated like so much smoke without fire. Perhaps hoping to revive that possibility with another illegal venture into forbidden territory (however foolish the impulse), or maybe thinking to take the spotlight off Damien's discomfort, Ravyn prompted, "The wolves? Should we go back? I mean, we found tracks. And now that we know the police weren't after Damien..."

"Tracks?"

But Stacy overrode Bianca's question. "For freakin' real?" Her voice was so loud both Ravyn and Damien leaned away from it a little. The pleased smile on Damien's face quickly faded, however, as Stacy continued. "Cuz I wasn't picking up anything on the surveillance app."

"What surveillance app?" Damien's voice, though soft, was clear, each word distinct.

"That satellite tracking thing the biologists use." When silence still hung heavy, Stacy added, "You know: dart, collar, track. You can enter the site and see all the data from the collars anywhere in the world. In real-time. Thermal surveillance. Biometric data. No animal privacy at all. They even analyze DNA from the blood of ticks and mosquitoes to track the animals. Though they can't do that remotely yet. No wolves in the Bro Forest though. Not on the app anyway."

Ravyn wanted to hear more, but Bianca firmly interrupted as Stacy drew a breath. "Spring will be best, Ravyn. There was a report sent in about Damien, *sans* his name, of course."

"The police?" Damien asked.

"Yep, a police report," Stacy threw in. "But filed by private security. Something about a man in the Bro, ponytail, tall, difficult to track. And close to some military reservation. Or something. I don't know. My French isn't great, but the details I could understand fit you pretty close."

Damien nodded. "The military training camp is where it happened – security found my trail. But we're on to something, I think. Ravyn found wolf tracks by the camp, only miles to the east of where I was."

Ravyn's eyes grew wide. She hadn't realized she'd come anywhere near the military training grounds.

In the background, Stacy was strident in her protest. "It's not that I *like* wildlife surveillance." Her voice carried clearly. "I'll tear a radio collar off a wild animal any day – "

"Whoa. Okay." The somewhat muffled voice, not a little condescending in tone, sounded like Trevor. "Pause game. Exit eco-warrior mode. We all know you're nuts about this tech stuff."

There was a dull thud in the background.

"Sorry. As I was saying," Bianca began. "Just be sure to send me the story asap, Ravyn," Bianca finished. "Write in the wolves so they and the fairies are safe. And we'll call it good until Spring."

Though she didn't know how writing a story about the wolves would keep them safe, she had another more immediately pressing concern. "Um, with the fairies…" But Ravyn wasn't sure how to proceed next. She could admit there clearly was something going on at La Roche, but she was nowhere near convinced that little magical flying people were it.

As if sensing her reluctance, Bianca suggested, "Maybe use Damien's perspective on the fairies."

Gaze sidling to Damien, Ravyn raised her eyebrows in question.

"Of course," he said with a pleasant smile.

Lowering her eyelids, Ravyn hid how pleased she was he'd agreed so readily.

"I apologize," Bianca was saying. "This turned out to be far more complicated than we planned. And with so much that had to be left undone." There was a small silence. "I don't mean to pressure, Ravyn, but have you given any thought to your decision yet?"

Looking from Damien to the phone, the weight of the attention riveted on her next words felt almost palpable. A big part of her wanted to say yes. Despite missing the comforts of home. The certainties of each day's schedule. The cozy quiet of her pleasantly homebound life.

But what if she were to say no?

Nothing she couldn't travel on her own. Albeit in greatly simplified style...and without all the crazy security stuff that seemed to go hand-in-hand with MegaLit. Travel would be much more infrequent, at least when it came to the visiting foreign lands bit. But there was a lot to say for traipsing around the world with Pyxi – well, probably just the continent – in her little rust bucket. Her mom and dad dropping in now and then, adding an eccentric flair.

There was great appeal in all that.

But there was great appeal in the new possibilities before her too. Not without a little trepidation, she bit her lower lip, eyes wandering to meet Damien's. The dark gray she saw there deepened before he averted his gaze, thumbs tapping against each other.

The color of his eyes, so like the wolf from her dream, brought back the feeling of rightness she'd woken with that morning. The feeling of rightness she'd found in her walk through the wildwood.

Intently studying the carpet beneath her feet, it wasn't the pink shag she was riveted by but rememberings from the afternoon's time in the Brocéliande. A crow softly winging its way overhead. The smooth feel of the beech beneath her hand. Tiny green mosses, their tips sprinkled in dew. How they glimmered in the sun. The way they clambered down the roots of an overturned conifer, one of its boughs keeping secret the hidden track of a wolf.

It was magic.

The magic of wildness. An enchantment that was once felt, experienced, known everywhere. By everyone.

With a faint buzzing in her ears, Ravyn tried to nod, but felt a little too dizzy to pull it off and instead closed her eyes, feeling the hard pound of the pulse in her throat. Forcing a swallow, "Yes," she whispered before daring to look at the world again. When she did, the first thing she saw was a slow smile growing across her new partner's face.

"I'm sorry?" Bianca's voice sounded tinny and out of place.

Gaze locked with Damien's, Ravyn cleared her throat, answering firmly, "Yes. I accept the position."

Damien looked out the plane window.

Ravyn studied the blank screen of the phone.

"Good" was all Bianca said but she said it with enthusiasm. "Very, very good."

The relief that came once the decision was made surprised Ravyn who had, in part, expected a remorseful clench of the stomach or, at the every least, a sudden little onset of heartburn at the role she was taking on.

But then Bianca added, "Expect a few changes over the next few weeks as we get you more integrated into things."

"Changes?" Ravyn's voice lilted upward.

"Security things. Like getting you an air-gapped laptop asap. For your writing. Are you familiar with Linux?"

"Um." Pretty much the only things Ravyn had understood in all that were the words "laptop" and "writing."

"No worries." A mild clicking over the phone sounded like Bianca drilling her fingernails on that glass-topped desk of hers again.

"Our next assignment?" Damien asked, his smile rather surprisingly bashful as a he leaned toward the phone, avoiding Ravyn's eyes. "Any details?"

Bianca was silent a moment before she answered. "Something tells me the next one isn't going to come from me. You know how these things go, Damien."

Though Ravyn didn't, Damien evidently did for he simply nodded and sat back in his seat, his long legs in front of him.

"Ravyn, for now keep the story you're writing on paper only," Bianca added as if this was a logical follow-up to the previous topic. "Especially anything about the wolves. We'll have a secure laptop in the company vehicle when you get back stateside."

Ravyn acquiesced. Clearly this paranoia would be weaving itself into the very fabric of her life from now on.

When Bianca signed off, Ravyn and Damien fell into an awkward silence, the tension of which was only broken when Damien pulled out his book. With his attention diverted, the energy in the small plane relaxed. Ravyn grabbed her notebook, finding the ensuing atmosphere conducive to jotting notes for her first assigned story.

It was dark by the time Ravyn arrived back home, MegaLit's Escalade pulling up by the bare maples outside her front walk. Overhead, through wisps of cloud and the warm glow of street lamps, the brightest stars of the Big Dipper shone faintly. The trees held heavy snow. Vehicle tires creaked as they rolled down snowy streets. Someone had shoveled for her. Tall snowbanks lined the path to her porch steps.

Fumbling for her key – so long unused she had trouble remembering where she'd put it – Ravyn heard a soft mew from the other side then a gentle thump. Pyxi peered at her from the inside sill of the window near the door. "Missed you too, kit," Ravyn said, turning the key in the lock.

Crossing the threshold, it was dark and cold inside in a manner she'd not often experienced. Flicking on the light, even the plants in the entry seemed to sulk at Ravyn's abandonment, leaves droopy, soil slightly dry to her pinky finger.

But a soft and furry paw tapping her knee was all she needed to resuscitate the heart of home, laying neglected as it had for far too long.

The creak of porch boards announced Damien's approach behind carrying the rest of Ravyn's luggage. Pyxi, her tail lowering as she stood with one paw on Ravyn's booted foot, watched him with slanted green eyes. Then, after several moments, the cat picked her way to him and placed a paw on his boot.

Moving slowly, Damien crouched back on his heels, hand palm out to the little feline who soon acquiesced to a gentle tickle behind the ears, tail raising. "If you don't mind a walk through the house, it would be good," Damien said quietly...to Ravyn more than to Pyxi. Although by the way he maintained eye contact with the little cat, she was clearly also included in the conversation.

"You want a tour?" It's not that Ravyn was opposed. But, coats and all still on, it seemed like an odd time for one, especially coming in from such a long trip.

"Just a security check." His smile seemed tired but his tone was warm. "I don't mean to be weird about it, but, well, listen," he said catching and holding her gaze. "I want to know you'll be safe when I leave tonight."

Ravyn dropped her gaze to study the floor, smudging snow into the entryway rug as she worked to pretend the blossoming inside her was entirely due to rekindling the figurative flames of the home hearth. "If you think it's needed."

Damien left the bags and his snowy boots inside the entryway.

When they finished up the quick security sweep of her home – having found not a single intruder, not a window latch out of place – Ravyn looked sideways at him as he pulled his boots back on, zipping up his coat. "I'll call you when I'm ready to write the bit about the fairies?"

His smile seemed genuine. "Sure. It would be good, hanging out for a while."

She hadn't really intended it to be a meet-up, but it wasn't like she was going to complain. "Okay," was all she said, smile brighter than the LED lights of the Escalade waiting outside.

Within the hour – after a swiftly thorough clean up of the litter box, a measured watering of the plants (complete with murmured greetings and apologies), and a quick snack for both herself and Pyxi – Ravyn found herself finally slipping between cool sheets, burrowing into her favorite puffy comforter.

Pyxi purred, kneading her arm.

"Missed you, too, Pyx." Yawning, she leaned out of bed and pulled her backpack closer, its snaps scraping across the wooden floor as she brought it to her bedside. Rummaging for her writing notebook, Ravyn pushed through the detritus of the trip. Chocolate foil wrappers, empty bottles of hand sanitizer, a stray pen or two, and finally what she'd been looking for.

As she pulled out the notebook, something like an iridescent starflower glided to the floor nearly identical in color to what her father at found at La Roche.

It was blue. Azure blue to be precise about it. Dark edges limned the more translucent center. And it caught at the dim lamplight as a dewdrop catches the morning sun.

Swinging her feet to the floor, bare toes cold, Ravyn picked up the delicate, flowerlike thing, holding it loosely between two fingers. So ephemeral was it that even a grasp as gentle as hers crushed parts of it to powder, and Ravyn quickly lay it gently on her palm where it slowly continued to disintegrate from the outside in.

Tail curled round her haunches, Pyxi also watched in fascination. Ravyn held it closer for her cat to see, wondering how something so fragile had managed to make it intact thousands of miles in her backpack. Eyes crossing, paw hooked, the cat's front leg extended slowly, tentative but eager to touch. Then, with as gentle a caress as Ravyn could wish, Pyxi dipped her paw into Ravyn's palm.

Not unexpectedly, the dainty little thing crumbled into a powdery dust. A million glittering fragments of brilliant blue rose as if in a small updraft. Then dispersed.

It was certainly most familiar.

Pyxi batted at one of the stray and sparkling motes. Then all were gone, winking out as briefly as they'd arrived.

Tucking cold feet back into the warmth of her bed, Ravyn slipped the notebook on her nightstand for any nighttime inspirations, turned off the lamp and, eyes already closing, nestled against the familiar pillows. Pyxi curled into the crook of her arm, piquant feline chin settling with a quiet purr on top of Ravyn's hand.

It was good, so good, to be back home.

With a soft sigh, Ravyn burrowed under the warm blankets, snuggling into all the usual comfortable positions as sleep approached with quietly padding footfalls.

All remained almost perfectly still.

So still, one might hear a pin drop.

Or, with the ears for it, a snowflake fall.

Lingering within the reach of sleep, Ravyn was only vaguely aware that somewhere outside the frosted window panes, beyond the muted streetlamps' glow, a wild starlit darkness called.

"Come. Now, it is the time to know."

Ravyn flung open her eyes, sitting upright, unable to say for sure whether she had actually heard anything. Or simply dreamed it.

Irregardless, for the moment at least, sleep had withdrawn.

"Fairy frogs," Ravyn grumbled with a toss that sent Pyxi stalking to the foot of the bed. Gripping the pillow tight, Ravyn wrapped it firmly round her head, eyes shut – or almost – to the world just outside her familiar walls.

Book Two

DREAMINGS

Nateera Skye's Wild Magic Series

A dream.

An ancient land.

A man
she has yet to know.

On the threshold of a world
she has yet to understand.

COMING SOON

CRANBERRY FALLS &XXX
Book One

A Wildwood Romance

NATEERA SKYE

Nature photographer Natalie Reid has finally found independence...

...and she's far from ready to relinquish it.

Loving life as a single mom and nature photographer
in the heart of Michigan's beautiful Upper Peninsula,
Natalie has no time for romance.
Even when handsome local fishermen
maneuver themselves into the picture.
But will a run-in with wolves
be just the thing
for her change of heart?

Probably not.

NATEERASKYE.COM